DEAD ANGEL

DEAD ANGEL

JACK DOLPH

COACHWHIP PUBLICATIONS

Greenville, Ohio

To Eddie Dolph . . . whose lean and moving writing I commend with pride—and a touch of frustration—to tomorrow's publishers.

J.D.

Dead Angel, by Jack Dolph
© 2020 Coachwhip Publications edition

First published 1953
John ("Jack") Mather Dolph, 1895-1962
CoachwhipBooks.com

ISBN 1-61646-502-6
ISBN-13 978-1-61646-502-5

1

They tell me that, on his way to the chair "Little Willie" Angel fought like a cat—that his screaming seemed less that of a terrified man than of a frustrated child, unused to restraint.

I might have guessed he'd go out that way—but I didn't. It had been only a few months since he'd come scratching and screaming at me one unpleasant night, but I rather expected him to approach his death more as he had approached his life—at least most of it—a man with a considerable understanding of the major rules.

When I had last talked with him, he had accepted the fact that the State had to get rid of Little Willie in one way or another. Perhaps he was not quite prepared for the decision of the learned gentlemen whom his attorney quaintly called "alienists"—that Little Willie would have to go the hard way.

It was their considered opinion, presented in full force to a wavering jury, that Willie could not be destroyed without also destroying the physical body of the agreeable man within whom he had so long resided.

Sic transit Willie . . .

MONDAY EVENING, OCTOBER I
I seem to be involved in some sort of minor mystery. Three times, now, in as many days, a persistent intruder has entered and searched the adjoining apartments which make up my office and living quarters.

In our end of town we take petty pilfering pretty much in stride. Broadway and Forty-eighth Street pinpoint an area where the broke and helpless rub tattered elbows with sharply tailored percentage men and well-heeled sightseers.

But this is no petty pilferer. He's apparently neither broke enough to be interested in my old cigar box containing sixty-seven dollars of Clinic money—nor hopeless enough to make off with my modest store of narcotic drugs. He seems to have conducted his explorations in a most leisurely fashion, neatly replacing everything he's touched and leaving behind him the unmistakable fragrance of excellent cigar tobacco.

Perhaps I should explain here that the use of the term "clinic," or such expressions as "clinic money," shouldn't be taken too seriously. Both are thumping euphemisms dreamed up by the peerless Katie Storm for a sort of bi-weekly mass meeting of the neighborhood which occurs on the premises. The thing started with the janitor's self-inflicted gastritis and has since parlayed itself into something of a production.

These Tuesday and Thursday free-for-alls have the advantage of keeping Katie hopeful that my uselessness is not permanent. Their disadvantage, of course, is that I am being slowly but inevitably pushed back into the general practice of medicine— a dedicated business any way you look at it—before I'm ready for the cornerstone.

The sons of country practitioners don't have too many illusions about what happens to a physician from the time he hangs out his invitation for all the sundry to come and be healed. All the Old Doc ever owned in his long life, as nearly as I can remember, was his house, an old Ford, a saddle horse, and his fly rod. The rest of him was the highly prized but rather shabbily used property of an affectionately selfish community.

So, since being sprung from four years of military surgery which, I've been assured, presaged great things to come, I've declared a moratorium. The breather has now stretched into several very happy years during which I have courted Katie, from slightly afar, and romped around with a very stanch pal, the stalwart Edward Quinn Marsh, Lieutenant of Detectives, N.Y.P.D.

The by-product of my association with Katie has been a certain determination to settle down to a fine East Side practice—sometime. My romping with Marsh has resulted in a warm friendship—and a series of mystery stories which have, surprisingly, found their way into print.

As for the Clinic money, it is a highly fluid sum which is disbursed in four-bit to two-dollar dribs and replenished, on occasion, in larger amounts by certain of the local gentry who insist on invading the premises. Their principal complaints are hangovers, incipient paunches, and minor cardiac disturbances largely conditioned by too many photo finishes.

To these I minister tenderly, if extortively. They are admitted on Clinic mornings without regard for our traditional first-come-first-served policy and are occasionally presented to the assembled as Patrons and Trustees of the Clinic. Some of the better known get a hell of a hand.

Once admitted, they receive nothing but the best—generous helpings of intravenous vitamins for all and splendid A.M.A. diet sheets with one blank side for figuring mutuel prices. If there's anything much wrong with them, I send them over to Ralph Pack, who is much more enthusiastically concerned than I with the complexities.

In moments of extreme stress, I have been known to snitch an occasional buck from the Clinic money, but a small avuncular annuity and irregular checks from publishers keep me honest most of the time.

What is keeping my visitor honest is beyond me.

The fact that he is neat, has no interest in the money or drugs, and apparently smokes imported cigars disqualifies all the regular customers. Most of them are distinguishedly untidy, all of them are broke, and whatever odors they leave behind them are not those of expensive tobacco.

The thing started on Friday night when I came home from the fights determined to make a start on an overdue manuscript.

I sat down at the typewriter with a very fancy plot, a ringing title, and, characteristically, no paper. I went through the kitchen to the office apartment to get some.

First thing I noticed when I turned on the lights was that my accumulated third-class mail had been neatly piled on the desk. Mrs. Parter had swamped out on Tuesday, but three days of pharmaceutic bombardment in these times of strenuous competition for the patient's buck make a considerable mess. I was wondering whether I'd responded to some sort of peripheral suggestion and neatened the place up myself when it struck me that my cabinet door was closed. I leave it open, this time of year, for ventilation.

Then I noticed the cigar odor and looked for ashes. My tidy visitor had left none that I could find. I'd emptied the ashtrays Thursday morning after Clinic. I checked the money, the drugs, the door.

The locks in our old building are uniformly casual. Anybody who has a stiff celluloid card or, if he wants to be professional, a thin palette knife, can get around the place much as he pleases. The hall door was properly closed and latched as I'd left it.

Nothing, as nearly as I could tell, was missing. I made certain the guy hadn't invaded my living quarters and shrugged it off for the night.

On Saturday I didn't think too much about it because I went to a ball game with Eddie Marsh and had a date for dinner with Katie. However, while I was thus pleasantly engaged, the prowler dropped in again.

This time he had worked my bedroom over—with special attention to drawers, closet shelves, my luggage, and my bed. As on the previous night, he had left everything in unaccustomed order. The remade bed sported corners that would have done credit to Polyclinic.

The whole thing seems a touch critical of my casual housekeeping. Perhaps he is critical, too, of my conventional possessions. Again, nothing appeared to be missing.

I had a flickering notion to call Eddie Marsh—gave it up because the big cop would either fill the place up with precinct

men or—and/or—rib me for months about having to holler for
help. I hadn't mentioned it to Katie, either, because she would
have related the prowler to some former cops-'n'-robbers adventure with Eddie and indulged in a wholesome task. There might
just have been something to that, of course.

In the four years I've played unofficial water boy to the
Lieutenant's homicide team we've met some notably undesir-
able citizens. The circumstances wouldn't fit any that I could
remember, however. While some of them could afford to pass
up the sixty-seven bucks or disdain the drugs, there wasn't a
bedmaker in the bunch. Most of them held extreme views about
my interference with their respective ways of life but none, so
far as I knew, was particularly concerned with my own.

I think that, at that time, I may have been intrigued. At the
moment, I am just plain annoyed.

Before I turned in, Saturday night, I spent a vexing quarter
hour in trying to review everything I have—either here or in the
box at the bank—which might conceivably have sponsored such
a dogged hunt. It was a complete blank. I am not a complicated
person and dislike involved deals which, once undertaken, keep
haunting one's most casual thoughts. That goes for mortgages,
time payments on cars, unanswered letters, and promises to
get somebody a job. Neither am I a preserver of old letters and
other highly intimate souvenirs. Beyond a fairly orderly drawer
of canceled checks, there are few evidences of my personal
affairs around.

Whatever the man is looking for, I haven't got it.

But he keeps drifting in and out of the place at hours carefully scheduled to my unscheduled comings and goings! Of
course getting into the building wouldn't be so hard. The street
outside is usually full of people, but the busy are too busy and
the aimless too aimless to be much concerned. The lock on the
lobby door is no better than those inside. You could poke a
quarter through the interstice between door and frame.

Once inside, an intruder could wander around almost at
will. Paddy, our janitor-manager, has never been known to
crawl from his hole unless vigorously summoned by name. As

nearly as I can make out, Paddy is engaged in a permanent pinochle marathon, supported in relays by a well-organized force of neighborhood challengers.

Even the two doors of my office and living apartments—together with the stairway to the lobby—afford a sort of cat-and-mouse choice of escape routes, and the old elevator would rate an assist by clanking out the threatened arrival of any legitimate visitor.

I think the thing that made me most angry at my cigar-smoking guest was that he seems to have used all these factors with complete assurance. He must have spent hours in the place.

On Sunday morning I kept a long-standing date with Johnny Fitz at Aqueduct. The yearlings are well broken by early October and have commenced their long, slow period of conditioning—a period during which most horsemen allow themselves to do a little wishful thinking. At least people like Johnny and I do. Maybe Mr. Fitz doesn't. He's seen a lot of them come and go in his more than fifty years of horse training. I wonder if even so experienced a hand is immune—especially one who has seen a Gallant Fox, a Snark, a Seabiscuit, or an Isolator emerge from under his October eye.

Anyway, we inspected the youngsters and had fun. I'd decided to get back early and lie in wait for my intruder—just in case the thing was getting to be a habit with him. If it hadn't been something of a major accomplishment to get Johnny to the track on a non-work day, I'd have called it off. As it was, he had to be in Sheepshead Bay before eleven and I was home before noon.

The intruder had come and gone.

This time he'd been through the living room, with special attention to my personal desk. A dozen small signs of his activities led me through drawer after drawer—a knotted rubber band which had, apparently, been broken—the paper lining of one drawer torn and discarded in the wastebasket. That sort of thing.

It's a creepy feeling—made rather more so, I guess, by the recentness, the afterimage, suggested by the still fragrant cigar smoke. The living-room desk, too, is pretty close to home.

Somehow, the desk in the adjoining apartment is something else again. It's filled with other people's problems—professional observations and records comfortably removed, in their orderly files, from the parade of human miseries that prompted them. Whatever he may have found in my personal desk may have been dull reading, if he bothered to read, but it was still too close.

I decided, then, that I'd be waiting for him if he came again. That's what I am doing right now. Tonight I went across the street to a restaurant where I am well, if not favorably, known for once having pursued a cat through the place. I entered, looked around, and moved back to a point where I couldn't easily be seen from the street window, prowled through the kitchen, and out into the alley at the back. From there, I skulked through Forty-eighth Street and into my building by the janitor's door. I didn't light a light until I'd weighted the shades down—and then only the small one over the desk. I'm even writing this blow-by-blow account with a pen—a process which I dislike intensely—to still the resounding clatter of my old Underwood.

No sale. Maybe he's found what he wanted. Maybe he's just plain smart. It's all very unpleasant.

I'm not good for much longer tonight. Tomorrow's the Clinic again and I'm about due for some new air in here. I must be on my third or fourth round of this stuff. I'm getting punchy.

If he's found what he wanted, he's welcome to it. It certainly isn't anything of value to me! If he hasn't found it I wish he'd get at it and go home. I don't intend to spend the rest of the week locked up in this apartment—and I certainly have no intention of filling the place with cops. Eddie Marsh has few interests in life beside beefsteaks and corpses—the steaks large, well aged, and rare—about the corpses he shows considerably more catholicity. Eddie sides warmly with Katie in disapproving my residential area, my acquaintances, and my habits. I suspect he would enjoy making the most of a deal like this—a slapstick production which would end up in the local columns.

Tomorrow, as soon as I get shed of the Clinic, I'll go to the races and give my non-stealing burglar a free hand. Maybe after he's got it I can find out what he wants. Maybe, if I can find out what he wants, I can find out who he is. Then maybe I can poke him in the snoot and tell him to stay off my preserves.

I think I'll leave him a friendly note to lower his guard. Let's see! How would it go?

> Dear Nosey:
> Five will get you ten I haven't got what you're after, but make yourself at home, anyway. Don't thank me, it's been no trouble at all. You've been so neat about everything. If the condition of the living-room rug offends you, you'll find the vacuum cleaner in the hall closet.
>
> Doc Connor

2

A light Clinic got me away early to the races. I've observed, for whatever it may be worth to the Department of Public Health, that the imminence of a World's Series always conditions a surge of well-being around our neighborhood and even the steadiest of complainers shows signs of euphoria. As a result, I had time to get to the clubhouse soon enough to find a good seat and have lunch pleasantly on the upper terrace. To the uninitiated I might explain that this is accomplished by promising the head-waiter that you only want lunch and that you'll get the hell out of there before the heavy-tipping regulars arrive, around the start of the first race.

I was working on some clams and trying to get a glimmer out of the *Telegraph* when Truck Snowden waddled over. Truck is a very sound horse trainer—a fat man who came down from Toronto, some years ago, with a likely-looking colt called Black Lancer. Snowden won a couple of minor stakes with him and promptly sold him for a substantial sum. The colt has long gone from the racing scene, but Truck has been around since, apply-ing his talents to a public stable of race horses and owners of varying degrees of quality and resource.

For the last couple of years, Snowden's principal client has been the Angel family—five brothers and a sister whose Cuban sugar cane grows tall and sweet by cabled command from New York.

The big fellow wheezed his way over to my table, sat down, and refused a drink. "Doc, I been hopin' to run onto you. When I saw you comin' in, I chased you up here. I need to talk to you."

"Good. What's on your mind, Truck? Want me to prescribe a diet, maybe?"

"Why, damn your presumptuous heart! You ain't had enough practice since I've known you to treat bee stings!" His big face rolled into a happy pattern. "Now, if I had a bad-legged horse . . ."

"You never had anything else—not of your own, anyway."

Snowden squinted his eyes at me and chuckled—a massive process concerned largely with his viscera. "Never could afford to own any but the sort the other feller give up on. Still and all, I've not done too bad patchin' 'em up."

He hadn't either. Give him a knotty-kneed plater with a touch of class and Truck would walk him into shape—let him play on the end of a lunge line, breeze him a couple of times, and beat good horses with him.

They call them gyp trainers around the track because most of them gypsied about the frying-pan circuit—the fairs and the half-milers—before they hit the big apple. But don't sell them short. The gyps embrace some of the most astute trainers in the business.

As to my own love of horses, it started the day the Old Doc gave me my first pony—no shetland, that one, but a tough little thoroughbred Irish hunter named Mr. Arbuthnot who could jump a foot higher than his withers.

I'm a fair country hand with a bad-legged horse, myself.

"Doc, like I told you, I've been hopin' you'd be out one of these days—it ain't anything too serious, but I've got something on my mind you might help me with—if you felt like it . . ." Snowden was almost childish in his huge shyness.

"Well . . . I've done things for people I liked a lot less, Truck."

He broke a roll in his heavy hands and grinned. "I know." Then he sat for some time—glancing here and there along the pavilion like a man looking for a friend. I went on with my lunch and waited him out. Finally he said, "I thought so . . ."

"Thought what?"

"You remember Joe Hernandez, Doc?"

"Joe? Sure. I knew him well on the Coast. Why?"

"I was about to quote him."

"Oh?"

Truck pudged a thumb over his right shoulder "'. . . and here comes *Malicious!*'"

I looked along the line of tables and saw Buzz Chapin coming toward us. "Who—Chapin? I take it you don't care too much for Buzz."

"He's a no-good heel. I knew he'd be over as soon as he saw me with you. Stand by for the touch, Doc—and don't let that two-hundred-dollar suit fool you. Whatever he's got to say will cost somebody."

I'd have guessed the suit at maybe fifty dollars more than that at the going rates. The gray shirt was something of a deal, too—collar points just enough off beat to show they were custom-made—generous rolled cuffs with square-faced links of burgundy enamel to pick up the color of the knitted tie. The whole outfit was flagrantly conservative. The guy had his hunting clothes on. He was working his trap lines.

"Well, gentlemen . . ." He sat down in our spare chair. "This is a great pleasure, indeed!"

Truck stiffened with some internal effort, then relaxed and belched—as though he'd saved the greeting for just such an occasion. "Chapin, on anybody else them clothes would look good."

Buzz smiled happily. "Don't be unkind, Truck. I was just about to tell you how nice you look with a coat on. Are you training from the clubhouse these days?" The man turned to me. "And what's with the Squire of Midtown, Doc? I've missed you from the public prints."

"A good thing, too. It was getting so my criminal friends wouldn't trust me any more. I've given up detecting for horse doctoring."

"Horses are simpler." A waiter ventured too near the table and Chapin tagged him for a double benedictine and brandy.

Snowden said, "What'd I tell you?" and went on chewing his roll. The public address system started announcing program corrections and our guest hauled out a splendid silver pencil and marked his card. The drink came and he sipped it absently between references to his paper work. The party got pretty dull and I was about to flag the waiter down for a check when Chapin suddenly decided to conclude his handicapping and be on his way.

He packed his stuff in various pockets and finished his syrupy drink. "Well, gentlemen," rising, "I have some people to see . . ."

Truck Snowden looked up at him. "No doubt."

"And Doc . . ." He adjusted the full, gray cuffs and snugged his jacket around his shoulders.

"What?"

"Hope you're keeping up on your judo."

If the guy had wanted me to give it a take he must have been pleased. "Judo?"

"Quite!" Chapin leered at Truck and then gave me some of it. "I've never bothered with the stuff, myself—but then, I've not had too much experience taking weapons away from enraged husbands."

He strolled away. I couldn't get my mouth closed in time to say anything until he had disappeared into the mass of women's hats and sweating waiters. Snowden was chuckling when I turned back to the table.

"You been enraging husbands, Doc?"

"What's the man talking about?" It didn't make sense. "He's nuts!"

"He may be nuts . . ." The big face was too serious. "You're the expert on such matters, my friend, but I can tell you one thing; he's dirty smart." Truck waved his fat hand toward the empty oversize cordial glass. "Whatever he's talking about, it'll cost you to find out!"

Enraged husbands! The crack had all the earmarks of an incipient shakedown. "You suppose the guy's trying to set me up for something, Truck? He doesn't make sense otherwise."

Snowden carefully shifted the other half of his broad bottom to the inadequate chair. "If I know Chapin, Doc—and I've had some reason to—he's already got you set up for something. If you haven't been enraging any husbands lately, I'd say you were just about to go to work on one. Maybe Chapin's timetable is off a little, but there'll be a husband in there someplace, right soon."

"It's silly, but I'm forewarned, at least." Enraged husbands! An enraged Katie would make the average embattled husband wish he'd stayed home. "What's Chapin do to acquire two-hundred-dollar suits?"

"Oh—right now, maybe Series tickets. This and that. Among other things, he annoys the Angels . . ."

"How?" Annoying Truck's meal ticket would strike him as very wicked, indeed.

"Hanging around, Doc—little things. Chapin likes to think he gets around with the best people and is willing to run errands and that sort of thing in exchange for a nod in a night club. It's that way."

"Still, he's a percentage man . . ."

Truck sighed and arranged crumbs on the cloth. "A mark-up man. I've watched him around for years. I'll bet when he was a kid and his ma sent him to the store, he had a deal on with the grocer."

"There are plenty of that kind around, Lord knows."

"Not like this one, Doc. I've watched those suits all the way up from twenty-two fifty. They ain't goin' to stop now unless somebody really hangs it on him good for once." The public address system blasted out and Snowden looked at his watch. "You figger on stayin' the card out?"

"I thought I'd leave after the sixth, Truck. Want me to hang around?"

"Well—no—I've got a horse goin' in the fourth, so I've got to get over to the back side now. I was wonderin' if you'd mind droppin' by the barn—like after the sixth."

"Why not? I'll be there."

"That's good of you, Doc. It won't take long." He heaved himself to his feet and dropped a couple of dollar bills on the table. "For Chapin's drink."

"Not at my table, pal. Wait a minute . . ."

"Let it stand, will you? I—owe him something." He started to splayfoot away—turned. "That horse I'm startin' in the fourth. He ain't in with much."

"Thanks."

I watched the wash of his broad wake to the end of the pavilion. The headwaiter gave my table a worried glance, so I called him over and asked for the check.

Back at the seat I'd staked out in the stand, I got to thinking of Katie—and enraged husbands—and Katie—and the sort of nasty scandal which guys like Buzz Chapin are capable of creating—and Katie. The apartment-searching episodes suddenly became important instead of simply irritating. Forty-eighth and Broadway is no place for a rest home, but too much was happening all at once even for our busy corner.

The first three races looked bad on paper and good out there on the race track. I researched Truck Snowden's horse in the fourth—found it was one of his own and, as I might have suspected, a leg job. The *Telegraph*—which records such pertinences—showed that the horse had not run since Florida and noted, along with the figures on his last race, the two most damning indictments in the book, "Pulled Up" and "Pulled Up Lame."

Betting on the trainer instead of the horse is strictly not recommended procedure, even when a legendary tendon magician like Truck is involved. On Snowden's "not in with much" suggestion, however, I had a mild flurry on the horse—a long, loose-quartered chestnut gelding which slept all the way to the gate and woke up when the bell rang. In case you have not been so informed, that is the preferred order. He was never headed and paid a cheery $38.80 for $2.00—$194 for my $10.

Having been thus rewarded, my passion for money play, never compulsive, was gratified, and I watched the next two races with more eyes for more horses than is possible when one has a bet riding.

After the sixth, I walked around to the back side. It's always a pleasant jaunt on race days—the ginnies hanging over the rail along the three-quarter chute where the lads whoop 'n' holler 'em out of the gate looking for a spot to run—the big-eyed, high-headed hots cooling out on the walking ring—the contrasting sleepiness of the barns where they're waiting for tomorrow, or the next day. It's racing, itself.

Truck's boy was still rubbing the winner when I got to the barn. The big fellow met me with a grin, too gracious to ask me if I'd bet on his horse. I gave the boy a five-dollar bill and walked back to Snowden. "He went nice, Truck. How'd he pull up?"

"Can't tell much about him till tomorrow, Doc, but right now it looks as if he come out of there as sound as a bell o' brass. I might do all right with him if I can keep him that way." He called out to the boy. "Run them heavy gray bandages onto him, Steps, and take him in. Might throw a light sheet on him for a while, too." He turned to me. "What say we go in the tack room?"

We walked between the neat rows of tack boxes and feed tubs to the screened door in the center of the outfit. Truck held it open and indicated the only chair in the little room—a massive affair which could have been designed only for the boss. I laughed and sat on the cot as he skillfully navigated the narrows and settled down in the chair. Then he laughed right back at me and began, I suppose, sorting out the right things to say. I used the interval to indulge in a little reverie of my own—the sort tack rooms always bring me—the associations of leather, of horse, hay, Bigeloil. After a while Truck said, "Doc, do you know Mrs. John Blair Ferrier, by any chance?"

"That would be Nita Angel?"

"Yes. Know her?"

"No. I'm a substandard risk in the station-wagon set. I've met Jack Ferrier around. Why?"

"She wants to meet you."

"What have I got that she covets? She looking for a new trainer, Truck? I might consider that . . ."

"You better come out and serve you a good, long apprenticeship before you start improvin' my horses, my young friend." He squeaked around in his chair, lifted an ankle with both hands to cross it over his knee. This feat completed, he sighed with satisfaction and beamed at me. "I wouldn't be surprised if she wants some high-class detectin' done."

"That's stupid!" It never fails. Somebody refers to me as a detective and, all of a sudden, I become a hell of a physician. "Didn't you tell her I'm a doctor, not a detective?"

He sorted his face into a huge, cherubic grin. "Now, Doc! You know I ain't well enough acquainted with you to recommend for or agin you at either job. I said, yes, ma'am, like always."

"You know what's on her mind?"

"No. And I don't want to. If you'll see her, I'm to call her and tell her so. If not, she'll be mad as hell. What can you lose? You might even get invited out to one of them big binges at Cielito down the Island a way."

"Would it mean anything to you, Truck? Professionally, that is?"

"Maybe not, Doc. Maybe so. I don't know. She's been off her feed lately and I know she's got somethin' on her mind that worries her. It might just be an awful nice thing for you to do, Doc—if you seen fit to do it."

"All right, Truck. I can listen to her anyway. I can't promise more than that."

He began to look squint-eye triumphant. "That's all you promised, isn't it?" Then he blushed.

Darwin would have added another chapter to his perceptive old book if he'd seen that blush. Last I saw of it, the vast phenomenon was disappearing below Snowden's low shirt collar and apparently spreading to areas undreamed by science.

"Yeah, Doc. That's all I promised."

"Go ahead and call her. She can fix it up." I got ready to go. My winnings were already burning in my pocket and Katie would be waiting to help put them back into circulation.

Truck struggled to his feet. "You're a pal."

"Want to tell me a little about the woman?" I didn't feel too happy about getting talked into something by a high-pressure female—and I'd heard her reported as such.

"Like what, Doc?"

"Oh—like how you know she wants some high-class detecting done. Or how you guess it." It seems to me there's no cagier guy in the world, by nature, than an open-faced fat man. You could just see the big lug puzzling like a striving child to think of some small thing that might be helpful.

"Well, come to think of it, she asked me quite a lot about your detectin'. Maybe that sort of gave me the idea . . ."

"I can see where it might, if you're sensitive to that sort of thing." You can't get mad at the guy, somehow. "Goddammit, Truck, what's she want?"

"I dunno, Doc." As we walked out and past the shed, he looked around us before he spoke again. "There's one curious thing, though. She's the second one in the family to ask me about you in the past week."

"Wait a minute! What's this?"

"Yeah. One of the boys called up—like a week ago—"

"Which one?"

"I dunno, actually—"

"That's silly!"

"Not with that family, it ain't. They just call up and start talkin'. Most of the time I know their voices. After I hung up I tried to figger which one it was. It didn't seem to make much difference at the time. He just sailed along like, 'You know this feller, Doc Connor, Truck? Good feller, is he?' I told him you were just a dandy feller and all, then he says, 'Good. I want to ask him a small favor. Thanks!' Then he banged off without another word."

"I see. So his sister asked the small favor instead. That could figure all right. He could have called for his sister."

"Sure. Or his wife. Ferrier talks like the rest of them. It ain't Cuban, their accent; it's some kind of Long Island."

I headed for town in a cab. The races were just about to break and I could have beaten the crowd to the trains, but cabbing home is an occupational disease with winning horse players and I'm no exception.

All the way back I had the disturbing feeling that Buzz Chapin might have been right—even if a little premature.

Maybe I'd better brush up on my judo, at that.

3

At six forty-five tonight, I dripped out of the shower to answer my telephone. It was Katie—bearing strange news. "You have arrived."

"Where have I arrived?" Katie's messages of import are always chopped up into bite-size tidbits—arranged for climactic delivery.

"You have arrived, my darling, at the end—the jumping-off place."

"This sounds long. I'm dripping—"

"From what I hear, that's appropriate enough."

"Look! I—"

"I've no curiosity for that sort of thing. Get your robe on before you catch cold."

"How many times have I told you that nobody ever caught cold—"

"Get going, friend. You are having cocktails tonight with the gay set."

I got a robe on and came back to the telephone with strange misgivings and lurking anxieties. I had a hunch Katie was about to join the parade and accuse me of enraging somebody's husband—which, as far as I was concerned, would tear it. "All right, let's have it."

"I have just hung up the phone from being invited—provided I bring you along—to have cocktails with Anita Ferrier. Why?"

"The roundabout approach, eh? How well do you know her?"

"Don't stall. *Why?*"

"She wants something of me. How well do you know her?"

"Edgishly. The wickeder end of my friends overlaps her some. What does she want of you?—and don't get smart."

"I think she wants some detecting done."

"You're not going to do it, are you?" Katie wasn't kidding.

"Probably not. I'm curious, though. Aren't you?"

She hesitated, savoring her curiosity. "Yes—a little. I suppose it's worth getting drunk once for. Seven-thirty, at their Park, if you please, Avenue duplex. Hurry over and pick me up. I can't wait!"

That's how, come eight o'clock, we were treading deep in the carpets of the rich, drinking hard, dry martinis, and nibbling at things I'd read about.

Jack Ferrier came in some time after we'd arrived and seemed, I thought, mildly surprised to find us there. He was gracious enough—a lean, pink and gray man around fifty. You could see the boots and breeches on him as he moved around in his dark business clothes and fell into unconscious attitudes of the horsy. His chatter confirmed my guess that he would have more use for course and show jumping than for the hunting field. We got along.

After a couple of cocktails, Ferrier muttered apologies about a business date for dinner and hurried off. It didn't seem prearranged. Anita Ferrier saw him affectionately away and came back to us—a very beautiful, poised woman of medium height and intense Latin coloration.

She was also an insidious pourer of martinis. No brandishing of shakers or bandying of halfhearted words—no fuss, no bother, and, zip, you're loaded.

That sort of thing had been going on for some time when she turned to Katie and announced the pay-off.

"Katie, dear, I'll have to confess, now. I've been using all sorts of subterfuge to make this appointment with Dr. Connor. Now I'm going to ask you if you'll give me five minutes with him. Can you meditate or something? I'm awfully sorry, but it's terribly important to me."

Katie to the rescue. "Take him along, of course, Nita—or do you want me to go someplace?"

"No. Stay here, by all means. We'll talk in the library if the doctor doesn't mind sort of singing for his supper . . ."

"I'm quite used to it. I hope it's something simple like a headache." I got up and waited in front of my chair. "I don't mind at all." It seemed like the right thing to say at the time.

She stood there and burned those black eyes into me before she smiled. For an instant, she seemed intensely serious. Finally she spoke.

"It's a headache, Doctor. I hope it's simple." We walked into the library—a real one with books. The only sets were old and titled in Spanish.

The furniture was in sharp contrast to the rest of the apartment. It was old and it was strictly grandee stuff with massive carved frame and patined leather wherever leather could be used. Anita Ferrier sat, as though by protocol, in a severe straight-back number and waved me to the papa chair.

She adjusted herself rather carefully and said, "Well!" Gathered her thoughts. "I've taken an unfair advantage of you, Doctor, but I know of no one else to whom I could—talk."

"Truck Snowden said something about it."

"I know. He called me tonight and said you'd kindly agreed to—what shall I say?—listen, at least. He was very careful to warn me that you don't undertake this sort of thing professionally."

"This sort of thing?" I don't know whether I felt like being helpful or challenging. "Is it an investigation of some kind, Mrs. Ferrier?"

"It is a personal problem, Doctor—and rather a touchy one. I should say it would be an investigation of some kind, yes." She frowned slightly, touched her cheek with her fingers. "There are cigarettes at your elbow."

I thought she was asking for a breather and fumbled around with the carved box—offered it to her.

"Thank you. For some reason, I never smoke when I drink anything." I think she was grateful for the minute's delay. "I suppose it's that I prefer to enjoy my vices separately."

There was no percentage in following that up, so I waited her out.

She half closed her eyes and watched me light my cigarette. When I'd settled back, she said:

"We are a large family—we Angels—and very—close-knit. I am the eldest and have been alternately teased, praised, damned, and spoiled by my five brothers. Do you know any of them, by the way, Doctor?"

"I think not. I've had them pointed out and all that, of course. They get around."

"Yes. They get around, as you say. We all get around. There's not too much reason why we shouldn't. Actually, we have been mildly useful, in a way. We have rather large interests in Cuba and we have accepted, along with our good fortune, certain pretty extensive responsibilities—to others who are less fortunate." She laughed without enjoying it. "But you see, I'm already apologizing for our uselessness."

"That strikes close to home, of course. I am constantly condemned for being useless."

"You'll perhaps understand, then. So. We are useless. My husband, on the other hand, is not. He is a very vigorous man. He is a broker of sugar and has known us all for many years both in Cuba and here." She regarded me thoughtfully. "My brothers do not like him."

"Openly?"

"No. We are well mannered together—only there is always an—undercurrent of ill will. My brothers, for instance, are devoted to our racing stable. Jack is openly critical."

"I thought I'd heard that your husband was a horseman."

"That is quite true. He is a superior horseman and keeps two fine hunters at Cielito, in Long Island, where we all have a country place together. It is simply that Jack feels that he earns his right to ride and that my brothers are wasters."

I felt I had to get someplace with all this. "If I may ask, where do you stand in the family feud?"

She hesitated. "I was about to suggest that it is not exactly a family feud, yet perhaps it is. And where I stand is very simple—

in the middle. Always. I love my husband and I love my brothers. I am uncritical of any of them—of anybody at all, in fact.
I wish only to live pleasantly. Lately, I have come not to care
whether we have our horses at all—whether my brothers waste
their income, and mine, or whether Jack has his way and we
withdraw from racing. As it is, my position is most difficult."

"You speak as though your own share of the—what is it—an
estate?"

"That's right. My share is the largest. My brothers could not
afford the horses without my bearing a large part of the cost."
Her smile was attractively rueful. "That is, of course, where my
husband's criticism is of—importance—to my brothers."

It would be. I decided I could be patient in finding out why
she wanted detecting done. "I see. Tell me. The question is
pretty intimate . . ."

"I understand, Doctor. There is much more to say."

"Is your income larger than your husband's?"

She smiled—a little bitterly. "You do find the sore spots! Yes.
Jack has had to earn his money. He has had to earn everything
he's needed to pull himself up from a very obscure beginning."

"Obscure? Just how do you mean that, Mrs. Ferrier?"

"As it sounds." She looked away from me. A maid rapped at
the door and brought in a shaker of martinis and some canapés,
announcing that Miss Storm had thought we'd need them. We
each took a cocktail as the maid set the tray on a bench and
retreated.

"Yes. Obscure is the correct word, I think. Jack suddenly appeared in Havana some twenty-three years ago with a terrible old
scow of a boat and a few dollars. He bought some sugar. Nobody
knew where he came from and, I suppose, nobody ever asked him."

"Have you?"

"Yes."

I waited and nothing happened. When somebody had to say
something, I said, "That's background, of course. Isn't it time
for you to tell me why you want me to investigate something?"

"I was getting ready to. I am convinced that one of my
brothers is attempting to blackmail my husband."

Just like that! "Which brother?"

"I—don't know. Actually, that's what I want to find out."

"But you have a suspicion?" I should have known better.

"It is to avoid the unfairness of what you call a suspicion that I need intelligent outside help, Dr. Connor. I do not wish to speak in riddles, but *any* suspicion I might have with regard to my brothers would be a most unpleasant thing. The suspicion I *do* have is unbearable. I shall not disclose it—at present, at least."

"Will your husband co-operate with—whatever investigator might try to untangle your problem?" I was about to suggest Elegant Johnson or some other competent personal-affairs detective, but I was still curious.

"My husband? Of course not. That's why I called Katie so hurriedly tonight. I knew he'd have to leave. He wouldn't admit such a thing—let alone discuss it."

"He hasn't discussed it with you?"

"Never! I think he'd rather take it to the police than discuss it with me."

"Then how do you know—or suspect—that he's being blackmailed by one of your brothers?"

She got up and walked over to the bookcases, removed a volume, and leafed it through. A folded piece of paper had been hidden between the pages. "This note."

The woman held the paper in her hand and crossed the room toward me. "For several weeks, now, my husband has been intensely worried—upset—about something. He has said nothing about it and, after asking him once what was troubling him, I have said nothing about it, either. He was quite emphatic about its being simply an office matter of no importance that was annoying him." She handed me the note. "Then I found this."

It was typewritten, all in capital letters like a telegram, on a plain piece of paper.

MY DEAR BROTHER-IN-LAW, THIS IS HARD-
LY AN AFFECTIONATE COMMUNICATION,
BUT I EXPECT IT TO BE AN EFFECTIVE

ONE. YOUR CONTINUED INTERFERENCE
WITH OUR AFFAIRS FORCES ME TO WARN
YOU THAT THE BOLADO MATTER HAS
BEEN THOROUGHLY INVESTIGATED AND
DOCUMENTED. YOUR HOSTILITY IS NEI-
THER JUSTIFIED NOR, UNDER THE CIR-
CUMSTANCES, PRUDENT.

That was all. No signature—wisely, of course. I turned it over. There was nothing on the back.

"May I take this with me?"

She thought it over. "I believe it might be better for me to keep it. I should not like to admit to my husband that I had given it to anyone. Our—relationship is such that, if he believed I had it, he might well wait for me to ask him about it." She smiled nicely. "Or does that sound dreadfully complicated."

"It sounds like a most happy arrangement between two very thoughtful adults."

"Perhaps you'll make some sort of a copy of it."

"The wording is enough for now. If things become—more acute, we can study the note itself for source of paper, typing, and that kind of thing."

I copied the text in my notebook. "Did this come through the mails, Mrs. Ferrier?"

"I have no idea. I found it carefully hidden under the lining paper of one of the drawers in my husband's desk. We were cleaning house after being away most of the summer."

"We? Ferrier doesn't suspect you have this, does he?"

"No. I'm sure he doesn't. By we, I meant Julie, the maid, and I. Jack's personal things were my job, of course."

"Didn't your husband miss it? Ask about it?"

"He apparently missed it but didn't ask directly. He grumbled about clearing out his desk and wanted to make sure I hadn't thrown anything of value away by accident. When I told him I was certain I hadn't, he seemed satisfied and said nothing more about it."

"Being quite certain you *had* thrown it away, of course."

"I suppose so. He would have thought that I was incapable of finding such a thing without speaking to him about it."

"And why didn't you speak to him about it?"

Anita Ferrier looked at me in a puzzled way—as though I should have known the answer to that. I should have. Patiently, "You see, Doctor, if there are—areas—of my husband's early life with which he is not happy, I wish only to destroy them—not discuss them."

"I take it from that statement that you don't care to tell me what the 'Bolado matter' is."

"Bolado is an old and honored Spanish name. It suggests nothing to me which might be a—threat to my husband." The black eyes came to life. "Please understand. I wish very much not to know anything at all about any part of my husband's life he feels he should withhold from me."

"It might be necessary to—dig it up, Mrs. Ferrier."

"I see, now, that you are bullying me, Doctor—perhaps with good reason, from your viewpoint. Let me assure you, I have nothing more to tell. The Bolado matter has already been dug up, whatever it is, and there are documents, somewhere, which apparently are considered dangerous to my husband's happiness—and mine. I wish them destroyed—unread."

"I understand." Only too well. "So you wish to—engage my friendly services, shall we say?—to find these documents and destroy them without knowing what I'm destroying?"

"You put it rather—pointedly." She shrugged without being extravagant about it. "Let's simplify it, Dr. Connor. I need help—and I can't tell how badly I need it because I don't know how seriously these—pressures—are intended. For the last week, I have been very thoroughly frightened. The men of my family are ordinarily quite casual and pleasant . . ."

The woman poured some of the ice-diluted liquid from the shaker into her glass—shoved it aside, slowly. She looked up again at me steadily, with the strange, inquiring look I was learning, already, to associate with her. "The men of my family have been spoiled. From childhood they—we—have had our way. We can be—destructively violent, Doctor."

I started to say something or other. A slight gesture of her hand stopped me. It was a small demonstration of exactly what she'd been saying. The gesture was pleasant—neither imperious nor impatient—yet it was final.

"Yes. I wish to retain your—friendly—services. I wish to retain them on any basis you desire. I do not wish you to do anything actually illegal or unethical. That sort of conduct would be very simple to buy from others. From professionals. I should not have come to you if there had been a less—embarrassing way."

"There's nothing embarrassing about it. I'm very fond of Truck Snowden and was glad to talk to you, first, for his sake." I felt myself getting into trouble, but kept right on with the process. "Now, two things bother me. One, I'm curious as the killed cat. Two, I despise blackmailers. Shall we talk it over tomorrow and see how I can help?"

"At any time you say. I'm deeply grateful." She stood up and held out her hand—a very graceful hand, indeed—surprisingly hard of palm. Maybe golf—tennis—bridle reins. As we turned to the door I suggested eleven in the morning at my place.

"I am spending the night at Cielito, Doctor, but I shall be back in town by eleven, surely." She put her hand on my arm, lightly restraining me. "There's one thing more, if you please . . ."

"Of course."

"I have had reason to believe that—one of my family might have tried to get in touch with you for some reason. May I ask if he has?"

"No." I gave a quick thought to telling her one of the family had called Truck Snowden—and checked it. If she hadn't learned it from Snowden, no use starting anything for him with his owners. "You are the only one."

She let her hand lie on my arm for a moment and stared thoughtfully down at the toe of her shoe. Then we went in to Katie.

That's the way I left it earlier this evening.

The way I left Katie, later this evening, was something else again. She was furious. I had, in her own phrases, kept her waiting for hours while a maid plied her with martinis until she was helpless and starving for something beside caviar—then ruined what might have been a very pleasant dinner by refusing to say one word—one word, mind you, about my prolonged assignation with Anita Ferrier. That sort of bullheadedness, of course, being the main reason why she wouldn't agree to marry me—*ever!*

4

It's just possible that everything I've recorded so far should be restated in other terms. Not the facts. They are relevant and, in any solution of this now dreadful mess, these facts must be essential. It's a matter of attitude. As I read back, it seems all very jolly and up-tempo and—I'm afraid—a little cute.

This adventure has ceased, very abruptly, to be cute.

It's vicious and dirty and degenerate. I can't escape from the conviction that I have been at least partly responsible in bringing about one of the nastiest acts I've ever known a human being to perform.

At some time between two and three o'clock this morning, Anita Ferrier was beaten to death by one of her brothers.

Over at the Tioga Village police station and downtown they are still making routine checks on Jack Ferrier and some of the servants, but they don't count. It's one of the Angel men.

I've met them all, now—five pleasant, gentle-mannered men, all approaching middle age, all grieving deeply over the death of the woman whom they had "alternately teased, praised, damned and spoiled"—and whom one of them had killed in an incredible fury.

Whatever bitterness I may have felt about getting myself involved with these people has given way to an intense desire to do something about it. Whatever amusement I may have experienced in setting down the facts as they have occurred up to now has given way to a grim feeling of the necessity for setting them down clearly and accurately. I'll start with my waking—unusually enough—at six-thirty this morning.

The thing that would not let me get back to sleep was a puzzlement over the fact that both Anita Ferrier and Truck Snowden had reason to believe that one of the Angel brothers was about to get in touch with me—or had already done so. Apparently my persistent visitor had believed so, too. He had certainly not been searching for one of his brothers or trying to get in touch with me. He had been trying to find something which, obviously, he thought one of his brothers had given me.

Even the most ardently scientific eliminator of coincidence would have given up after a whiff of the Havana tobacco left trailing around my apartment. Too many Cubans concerned.

The only point was that his brother hadn't got around to giving it to me yet. And that, of course, was why Buzz Chapin's husband-enraging schedule was off. He had known, apparently, that Anita Ferrier would be looking me up.

It had to be a physical object—this thing. The Bolado documents, whatever they were, would come naturally to mind after reading the blackmail note last night. I decided to think of the object as a packet of such papers—perhaps copies of letters, photostats, and that sort of material.

I was lying there being simple-minded about the thing when it occurred to me that such an envelope could have been mailed to me—a thickish, non-personal sore—and automatically tossed in with the mess of advertising stuff I get. I'm the most careless person in the world about mail—I receive so little that means anything.

The thought seemed worth getting up for, so I went through into the office apartment to look around once again. Mrs. Parter had come in after Clinic, as she usually does on Tuesdays, and the place was neat. There was nothing in front of the mail slot in the door. I sat down at my desk and shuffled through all my accumulated sales letters with their samples and stuffily worded brochures. Nothing. I chucked them into the freshly emptied wastebasket. Except the useful samples, which I save for the

Clinic. Every piece of mail in the place was exactly where I had left it—in a reasonably neat pile on the table behind my desk.

I took a last look around at the floor back of the table and found a white envelope. It was a plain, post-office three-center, addressed to me exactly as I am listed in the telephone book. There was no return address. Sharp creases indicated a considerable bulk of content. Two stamps had been added to the embossed one. It had weighed between two and three ounces.

It had been opened and either forgotten or discarded. The postmark clearly stated that it had been mailed from the main New York Post Office at seven-thirty on the evening of September twenty-seventh—a week ago today. The thing had been somewhere in my office for six days, yet the intruder hadn't found it—until when?

I hurried to the telephone and called Mrs. Parter. She'd just come home from her night building-cleaning job. After denouncing me for being so sloppy with my mail, she proved her point . . .

"When I come in to clean up after office hours you wasn't home to complain, so I give the place a good goin' over includin' the radiators which I never get time to get at—"

"And you found the letter? A fat letter in a white envelope?"

"And I found the letter. It ain't the first time they've fell back there, Doctor. They get pushed off the table by all that trash you—"

"You found the whole letter? With stuff in it? Not just the envelope, Mrs. Parter?"

"Land sakes! If I'd saved every empty envelope I've found around! No. It was a big, thick letter—like an important one—so I put it right square in the middle of your desk."

"This was yesterday afternoon, now. Is that right?"

"It was yesterday afternoon, Dr. Connor."

That was that. I hadn't gone into the office since Clinic.

My visitor had finally made it! Right in the middle of my desk. Smorgasbord! He'd made his successful foray in the interval between Mrs. Parter's leaving and my getting back from the races, or while I was out later. It didn't seem to make much difference, although I did wonder if my visit to the Ferrier apartment might have suggested to him that I'd received the envelope at last.

But that was this morning. Now I believe that my carelessness with mail was at least a contributing cause of Anita Ferrier's death.

I went back to look at the envelope again. It could have been something completely innocuous—but it wasn't. Inside the envelope was a narrow strip of carbon flimsy showing the marks of a paper clip. It read:

ERRATUM: P9-li 16, Caesar Bolado

and it bore an undecipherable inked initial—the sort of scrawl one makes initialing the seventh carbon of a four-page contract.

I put the material carefully into a larger envelope and carried it back to my living quarters without so much as looking at locks or for evidences of the guy's presence. He'd been there and he wouldn't be coming back. Not for the envelope, anyway.

I got around to making coffee at about seven-thirty and was on my third cup when Eddie Marsh called.

"Doc! What the hell have you got yourself into?" Eddie wasn't kidding. He threw it at me.

"Hey! Take it easy! You sound serious."

"You'd damned well better start sounding serious, yourself, for once! What's with this Angel business?"

"Nothing that could get you jumping around like that. Anita Ferrier asked me to do her a favor last night. I can't see what . . ."

"And right after that she went out to their place on Long Island and got herself murdered."

"Good God! How, Eddie? What happened to her?" He started to yap back at me and I hollered. "Why? Why *Anita?*"

He slowed down and did one of his switches from friend to cop—which was the way I needed him at the moment. "You expected somebody else to get killed?"

"*Anybody* else! Who did it, Eddie?"

"How the hell do I know who did it? They've got the sher-iff's office and half the cops in Nassau County on it. Now they want me—and, brother, do they want you!"

"Look, Eddie, where are you now?"

"Precinct. You dressed?"

"Yes."

"I'll be over there in five minutes and pick you up. Be down-stairs!"

I went down and waited.

We'd jumped off that way a number of times—always with a sort of spiritual whooping and hollering that was good to feel—but this time I couldn't get with it. I kept thinking of the poised and beautiful woman who had said, "We can be—destructively violent, Doctor." Of the guy who'd pulled into Havana with an old scow of a boat and nobody knew where he came from. Of the damned documents, the destruction of which was all Anita Ferrier needed to be happy—and, perhaps, alive.

Eddie squealed his rubber out of Eighth Avenue and hauled up fast at the curb. "Come on, pal, jump!"

I swung into the front seat and we took off—with Marsh growling the siren—proof, if I needed any by that time, that he was upset. He dislikes sirens and police officers who get a kick out of using them. I said, "How was she killed, Eddie?"

"She was beaten to death with a club of some sort. I haven't got details." He wheeled into Park and south toward the tun-nel. "Maybe you'd better tell me what you know about it on the way."

"I can only hit high spots. There's a lot to tell—now that this has happened." I couldn't even get it related yet, myself.

"What do you mean, 'now that this has happened'?"

"Just what I say. There's a hell of a lot of little stuff that didn't mean anything yesterday—I'd better start with my talk with Anita Ferrier, last night."

Marsh grunted and hit the siren. "All right, Doc. You know what I'll need now, anyway. Let's have it."

Through most of Queens I let him have it. Because he couldn't use his old black notebook, he asked few questions—

assured me he'd dig it out of me, inch by inch, later. For once, in a deal with the big cop, I didn't have any reservations. No qualms about injuring the innocent bystanders. Without interruptions for detail by Eddie, I got through the whole thing, as it had happened.

We were just pulling into Tioga Village when I wound up and Marsh started around blocks. When he retraced one of them I got curious.

"What's the idea?"

"I can't find the police station and I'm goddamned if I'll ask anybody." He tried another turn. "Look, Doc, I've got no idea what we'll run into here. They hollered downtown for help and, because they wanted you picked up, I got the thing." He looked up a side street. "So that's where they keep it!"

As we hooked around I saw the station house. "Not much of a one, is it!"

"That's exactly what I mean. Any outfit this size hear that story of yours, they'd send you to the county boobery. There's probably enough physical stuff around to keep 'em busy until I can sort that mess you gave me into something approaching sense."

"Then I tell them—what?"

We slowed down and headed for the curb. "Start with Katie's call, Doc. They want to know why you were at the Ferrier woman's house last night. Keep it like that if you can."

A cop with uniform pants and a black alpaca coat came out to meet us. "Lieutenant Marsh?"

"That's right."

"This other gentleman is Dr. Connor?"

"That's also right."

"Cap'n Feeney wants me to show you the way out to the Angel place. I'll get my coat." He jogged back into the building.

Eddie goosed the motor. "Feeney's the local chief. I've got a notion he's caught himself a handful, or they wouldn't have borrowed me."

"The Angel family is rich—and spoiled. From what Anita Ferrier told me of her brothers, I'd say they wouldn't pay any more attention to a local cop than they would their gardener."

The guy came out again buttoning up his uniform. He hove into the rear and said, "My name's Lynch. Turn left at the corner."

I said, "The Angel property lie in the town limits, Lynch?"

"Some of it—some in the county. Sheriff's man is around. Body was found in the town part, though. Turn right next corner."

Eddie said, "That should be enough law for anybody. What's Feeney want of the City?"

Lynch thought that over carefully. "Well, I'll tell you, Lieutenant; Cap'n Feeney figures a cop is a cop and a deppity sheriff is a deppity sheriff . . . so he thought maybe the crime was committed in the city and the body hauled out here."

Marsh grinned. "Could it have been that way?"

"I dunno. I ain't viewed the scene. Keep straight ahead now."

A minute or so later we turned into some iron gates. A man sitting in a parked car nodded at Lynch and waved us on and we rolled up a drive through as beautiful a piece of grass as I ever saw. No lawn—not an inch of it. Every blade of it was enclosed by three-board creosoted fence and available for grazing horses. Off to the left I could see a course of jumps—timber, neatly winged with hedge.

The house we were apparently headed for didn't seem large. At least two other dwelling areas could be seen as we approached the top of the gentle hill. One was what looked like a very attractive cottage down by the barns. The other, with a pleasant porch facing away from the main house, spread across the top of a tremendous garage.

I could see at least seventy acres—all grass across the hill and ending, apparently, with a patch of woodland beyond. No tennis court. No swimming pool. Just horses and grass.

I've had dreams like that. I'm sure someone very nice dreamed Cielito.

But beautiful women who have been beaten to death should not be part of such dreams—and into this one Anita Ferrier's murder had intruded.

As we pulled up at the door of the main house a man in plain clothes came off the steps and waved us on. "They're down at the cottage." We kept going and, as we turned back of the garages and started to descend, I saw three brood mares, foals at their sides, standing together and gazing in wonder at the activity below. Five or six cars were parked at the little place. Eddie said nothing. I asked Lynch who lived in the cottage.

"That's the Ferriers' place. They spend more time here than in the city—or at least they did."

"Where do the hands live—the servants and the farm people?"

Lynch waved back to the garage building. "Hell! They got it better than the family. Regular club they got there—over the garage."

"How about the brothers? I suppose they have wives and families."

"Some of 'em have and some haven't. I dunno which ones. They all got places in the city, though. I know that. They come out here to ride or raise hell or what not. I guess sometimes they bring their wives." The guy leered and rolled down the window. "Here are the men you was expectin', Cap'n."

As we parked, a burly man with no hat and no hair to speak of walked over and shook hands with Marsh. "I'm Feeney. Glad you got here." He turned to me without addressing me. "This Doc Connor, Lieutenant?"

From that moment, I needed no further instructions from Eddie not to tell Feeney anything. Marsh laughed. "Yeah, Chief, that's the Doc."

"All right, let's go." The cop turned his back to both of us and marched heavily toward the cottage. I muttered such observations about him as came to hand. Eddie climbed out of the car and I followed.

"Nice fellow, Doc."

"Yeah. You may have to bail me out of the clink before he gets through with me."

"Take it easy. Be a good lad and I'll trim him down to size for you." We went up the steps into the house. The place was packed—uniformed police, plain-clothes men, and reporters. Eddie elbowed through after Feeney, who announced Eddie like a train caller—by name, title, and origin. Then he turned to me.

"An' Doc Connor, gentlemen. You can help us with some of the medical problems, Doc. We only got three medics here now."

I continued to burn. "Thank you, Chief Feeney, but it looks like you had enough help around here already. I think you called me out here as a witness, didn't you?"

"That is correct. We'll get around to you." He bulled his way into a step-down living room and we followed him.

There, in the sort of untidy heap that only the violently dead assume, lay Anita Ferrier.

5

A man came over to Eddie and me. "I'm Franco, Sheriff's Office. We thought you'd like to see her the way she was found. Some question of jurisdiction here, Lieutenant, so we hung around."

Another man came up to me as Eddie and Franco walked over to the body. "I'm Dr. Phillips, Dr. Connor—County." He smiled and we shook hands. "There doesn't seem to be anything very complicated or mysterious about this one, but help yourself. The Chief doesn't care for physicians as a breed, but show him one with police experience and he really bites."

"So it seems. Somebody probably stepped on his tail when he was a pup. How was Mrs. Ferrier killed?"

Phillips made a gesture of distaste. "Pretty horribly. Somebody used that—device—over there . . ."

Lying on a piece of newspaper a few feet from the body was a twitch.

Phillips followed my eyes. "You'd recognize that sort of thing, of course."

"Yes. A twitch."

"I had to be told."

A twitch is a device with which you restrain a horse. It's a stout piece of hardwood a couple of feet long and about the thickness of a hoe handle. Attached to one end is a loop of leather or soft rope which is used to circle the muscular flesh of a horse's nose. When the stick is twisted, the loop tightens on the loose flesh and forms a most effective restraint. A twitch may be used quite gently—or very cruelly—depending on the user and, of course, the nature of the horse to be restrained. It is seldom needed around a barn, though every stable has one in case of emergency, such as the painful treatment of injury or, with some animals, during the regular visit of the dentist.

Reversed, with the loop over the wrist, a twitch resembles nothing so much as a policeman's nightstick.

I asked Phillips if he had examined the body in any detail. He made a small gesture of futility. "Enough. Palpable skull fractures, certainly fatal in themselves, and more areas of contusion than you can count. The guy must have hit her over the head first—nobody heard anything, apparently—then beaten her until he was exhausted. You don't see too many like that."

I studied the woman's body for a while. "Tell me. Did you clean up the floor?"

"No." He paused in applying his lighter to a cigarette. "I couldn't believe it, either."

"There's not enough blood." Some, yes, but not enough. "She was not dead when she . . ." When she came from where? "Were there any spots anywhere else?"

"They say not. At least they haven't found any, yet." He said it almost as a question.

"Then she wasn't dead when she entered this room, but she *had* been hit over the head!"

"I'd say so."

A matter of jurisdiction! Damage to brain tissue—with or without actual fracture—is completely unpredictable. Anita Ferrier could have been struck over the head in Manhattan, the Bronx, or simply fifty yards away in the stables. Once the surface bleeding had stopped, she could have spent an indefinite amount of time at reasonably normal pursuits before she lost consciousness and died. No wonder Feeney had felt justified in calling for help from the City Police.

Phillips offered me a cigarette, which I took. "You want to examine her? I'm sure there'd be no objection . . ."

"Hell no!" I wanted to answer Feeney's questions and get on home. "Thanks, anyway."

Eddie walked over and joined us. I introduced Phillips. "I've told Feeney and the sheriff that I'd like to take you up to the main house with me while I talk with the brothers and her husband. They're all here, still."

"The others have talked with them already?"

"As much as they need to right now. It seems they had a family powwow last night and all the brothers stayed over."

That would be six men up there—the whole group with their enmities and with blackmail hidden, somewhere, among them. We climbed the hill back to the main house and went in.

Against the background of that beautiful, modern room with its great fireplace and its horse prints, I saw the Angel men for the first time. Jack Ferrier sat, slightly aside, with a highball glass in his hand. He did not look up.

The others were sitting and standing around the fire.

Eddie said from the wide doorway, "I'm Lieutenant Marsh, gentlemen, of the New York City Department of Police."

A balding, heavily made man with a black mustache came forward. "I am Ramon Angel, Lieutenant. We greatly appreciate your help—but all of us have affairs which need our attention . . ."

"I understand, Mr. Angel. We'll not keep you long. This is Dr. Connor." Ramon Angel didn't cross the distance between us—bowed. Eddie and I walked into the room and stood near the group at the fireplace. Ramon said, "These are my brothers. I hope you can speak to us all together, Lieutenant. It will save much time."

The four brothers acknowledged the introduction without warmth and without speaking. Jack Ferrier had crossed to us, shook hands. I said, "I'm terribly shocked, Ferrier—and so sorry."

He looked steadily at me. His eyes were exhausted and unresponsive. "I did not know of your—interest in criminal matters when you came to us last night." His voice was just audible. Eddie had moved toward the others and could not have heard. "I still do not know why you came. Why my wife wished to—call you."

I thought it over carefully—and fast. Whatever advantage I might have in keeping my own counsel, I decided to hold as long as I could. "I feel sure she wished to—look me over. Would you know of any reason she would want to consult someone of my—someone of my interests who was not a professional detective?"

"I would not, Doctor Connor—but . . ." He made a tragically simple gesture with his hand. "There apparently was a reason."

I was glad, then, that I'd kept my information to myself. If Ferrier was going to be secretive over the blackmail business, I'd take it more easily—and wait for an effective point in our relationship to bring it up. That sort of thing can be used only once, as a rule. I couldn't blame him for dodging the issue—if it could be suppressed without hindering the search for his wife's killer. I said, "I am sorry that I couldn't have helped prevent this. Truck Snowden suggested that Mrs. Ferrier had wanted to see me several days ago."

He showed no added interest. "It is completely beyond me. There was no one—*no one*—who could have wanted this for her, Doctor! It could not have been anyone we know—none of the family—anyone. It was a madman. A degenerate from some state institution wandering through the woods up there . . ."

He walked quickly away. Out of the room.

I crossed and sat down beside Marsh. Then I realized, for the first time, that the room was hazy with the smoke of fine Havana tobacco.

Eddie had his notebook on a small table. "I'm sure you will all realize the necessity for meticulous accuracy and care in setting down the facts concerning this brutal affair. I hope, too, that you will realize that we are not likely to be searching among a group of intelligent, normal adults for the perpetrator of it. We must, however, clear away all the obvious facts at some time during our investigation, and it seems best to do it quickly while you are all together."

Ramon, apparently the eldest, said, "Of course. It is our duty. In the meantime, I suppose every precaution has been taken to insure that the . . ."

He hesitated at the word and Eddie rescued him.

"I have assured myself that everything is being done that can possibly be of any help at this time." He picked up his pen. "Now, gentlemen, I wish to ask each of you two questions which, I realize, may have been asked before. If so, you will be able to answer them promptly and simply. The first is, where was each of you between two and four o'clock this morning. The second, what facts do any of you know about the relationship between your sister and any other person—anywhere or at anytime—which might have contributed to her being attacked with the intention of causing her death."

A slight man across the group spoke up. "By attack, Lieutenant, you leave out the possibility of—criminal attack?"

"I do not leave out that possibility at all. I suggest, however, that it is not ordinarily simple to name someone who might have a recognizable predisposition to commit such a crime on a specific person. I am searching for a lead to anyone who might have hated or feared Mrs. Ferrier. Which brother are you, by the way?"

"I am Mariano Angel—the youngest." He had a wisp of a mustache, stringy and black like his hair. As were all his brothers, he was olive dark. "I was sleeping in my room. The small room at the back of the upper hall. I heard no sound during the night." He paused thoughtfully and Eddie waited. "I know of no person who would wish to harm our sister."

The Lieutenant said, "Thank you, Mr. Angel."

Another spoke up. He was, perhaps, forty. "I am Juan Angel. I think it should be brought up and disposed of at once that we have been in the midst of a family quarrel."

There was mixed approval and growls. Jack Ferrier spoke from the doorway. I hadn't noticed him come back. "I agree, Johnny." His voice was restrained. "It all seems like such a lot of damned foolishness now!"

"Yes." Juan gestured to quiet the others. "I'm sure the Lieutenant will understand at once, and I'm going to talk about it right here and now, whether anybody else likes it or not!" They all finally shut up and let him have the floor. "Lieutenant Marsh, we have been bickering like a lot of children for weeks over whether we can afford a racing stable. I have no idea whether the servants heard us shouting here last night or not—but it was the sort of thing that only strongly bound families can do . . ."

Ferrier spoke again—leaning dejectedly against the door frame. "I'm more or less the objector in all this, Lieutenant. I've been pretty much on one side and my brothers-in-law on the other. It's a simple matter. The Angel family has maintained a racing stable for years, but since the death of the older generation my wife has had to carry by far the largest burden of the cost. I have objected. It could not possibly have any bearing on this terrible thing."

Eddie, very quietly but without implication, asked, "On which side was Mrs. Ferrier?"

Ferrier gestured to Juan. "I think I can fairly leave that question to you, Johnny—although you're the most violent member of the pro-stable faction." He grinned just a little—rather hurt and tired.

"She wanted only family harmony. She tried so hard last night to say that she didn't care one way or the other. Look what it got her!"

Someone in the room muttered, "God, yes!"

"Have you, Juan Angel, any idea who might have hated your sister enough to do violence against her?" Marsh spoke mechanically.

"I do not, sir. None of us does."

"And where were you between two and four this morning?"

"I was also asleep. I heard no sound. My bedroom is in the front suite with Ramon."

So it went on. Ramon, the eldest, and Juan confirmed each other's presence in the suite insofar as neither waking the other was concerned. Carlos, a lean, ascetic type of person with a politely hesitant manner, had slept in the middle bedroom on the north side and Alonso in the south bedroom across from him. Alonso was also thin, but a much more positive person than Carlos—quick and eager and, surprisingly, in this dapper group, slovenly in his personal appearance.

None of the brothers appeared to have any idea of what could have caused anyone to attack Anita Ferrier. Eddie dismissed the brothers and asked Ferrier to stay a moment more. He joined us by the fire as the others went out to their cars.

The Lieutenant smiled pleasantly at him. "Mr. Ferrier, I felt it would be easier for you to talk with us after the others had gone."

"Thank you. It will be."

"Captain Feeney has told me that you arrived here late last night and left immediately after the—family meeting."

"That's true, Lieutenant. I arrived about ten-thirty and left about twelve-thirty."

"You drove, of course?"

"Yes."

"Can you tell me why you did not stay here with Mrs. Ferrier?"

"I had an early business engagement in the city. Mrs. Ferrier wanted to ride this morning. She didn't have to be back in town until eleven."

"Do you know what she intended to do in the city at eleven?"

"She said something about the hairdresser's." Apparently she hadn't said anything about her engagement with me—unless Ferrier was being unusually cagey.

Eddie went on. "I see. Did you drive separate cars or come together?"

"Mrs. Ferrier drove out in her convertible. I didn't think to ask what time she arrived. I believe they all had some sort of a pick-up supper together. I drove what we call the 'family car' to a dinner engagement and out here."

"Then you were at your New York apartment between two and four this morning?"

"Yes." He smiled—again tensely, but a good effort. "Of course, from the police point of view, I have no way to prove that."

"There are probably lots of ways to prove it—when we need to." Eddie closed his book. "Now tell me, Mr. Ferrier, why did your wife want to talk with Doc Connor, here?"

"She has never mentioned Dr. Connor's name to me that I know of. Except for what happened here last night, I'd have thought it was simply a social matter—a cocktail invitation to a young woman for whom my wife felt considerable admiration—Miss Storm. That Dr. Connor should be asked along would seem quite natural."

"But as it is, you might feel that she wanted something less impersonal of him? After all, they also had a common interest in horses. Could it, in any way, have had to do with that?"

"She was surrounded by people who knew horses pretty well, Lieutenant." Ferrier shook his head slowly. "It seems strange that, if she had any premonition of—trouble—she wouldn't have spoken of it to the doctor last night."

I said, "Doesn't it!"

The man looked at me without implication, but I was absolutely certain that each of us knew the other was lying. However. I felt equally certain that neither of us knew why.

6

THURSDAY EVENING, OCTOBER 4

The rest of yesterday was without progress and, to me, without interest. I escaped from Feeney and the bulky seminar of town and county representatives before having to account for my conduct previous to Katie's invitation to cocktails at the Ferriers'. I didn't escape a number of scathing cracks about my unofficial police activities, however, and my stanch supporter and friend, Marsh, became busy with other matters whenever the baiting got under way.

Don't let me poison your mind about Eddie. Permanently, that is. It was just his morning to be something of a bastard. The guy is most humble about rendering credit where credit is due—in his personal life. But try to take any kudos from his blessed department and he never saw you before. Any defense of my efforts would have had that effect.

Altogether, the several hours we spent at Cielito became increasingly annoying to me as they dragged along. I have considerable respect for the painful processes of research and have even been known to perform them when necessary. There's nothing in the book that says I have to like them. The interminable columns of distances from here to there, the patient hour after hour of patterned search for a drop of blood by orderly files of men on their hands and knees, the equally patterned questioning of a frightened handful of farm and domestic employees.

Fingerprints—there were, as you would expect, a lot of them around. Perhaps they would point out the killer and that would settle my part in the case. There were no recognizable prints on the twitch where they would have been most useful. Its irregular surface had been smeared or crudely wiped. The police would sort the prints they found neatly into a small catalogue of As, Bs, and Cs carefully noting where each had been discovered. At some later time, they would respectfully request names for them.

After we left Cielito, I went with Eddie to the Precinct where I unloaded every possible detail of my connection with the Angels to be officially; but privately for the time being, noted in the file. At several points in our talk I tried to get Marsh off into the implications of the murder rather than its physical facts. We have, on at least one occasion, popped off on a tangent with success. Not with this one. The Lieutenant, performing as he was under the noses of two outside law enforcement agencies, set about being even stodgier and more methodical than usual. He gave me the patient "all in good time" dialogue which he knows annoys me.

I came home and brooded and, as you know, wrote.

Tonight, as I write, the physical facts have come no closer to pointing out the degenerate killer of Anita Ferrier, despite the discovery, this morning, of what the authorities call the most vital clue in the case.

Eddie came in just before Clinic and had coffee with me— bringing, as he always does on such occasions, a container of orange juice and a tiny bottle of "store" cream. He had been out at Cielito and back.

After the brew had been set up on the kitchen table, he stretched out his long legs and grinned at me. "You will be interested to know, my friend, that from here in my concern with the Ferrier matter will be purely academic."

"How come?"

"I've been sprung. The crime was committed well within the limits of Tioga Village. Your friend Feeney will be very much upset when he finds out how much you have held out on him!"

"Wait a minute! How do you know where the crime was committed?"

"A rat ratted on the killer."

"Don't be coy! What happened?"

Eddie had a story to tell and he was damned well going to tell it his way. "I'm not kidding, Doc. Feeney's dopey lad, Lynch, was nosing around the barn after it had been searched expertly for hours—you know how they worked it over."

"She was killed in the barn?"

"Take it easy. This is one for the book. Literally. Reach over and get the pot, will you?" So that had to go on, complete with cream and four tablespoonfuls of sugar. "Anyway, Lynch is going over the barn when he spots something gray down a hole. Guess what!"

"The rat."

"No. The rat had pulled it down the hole with him, but what Lynch saw was a gray scarf—bloody as hell."

"She'd worn it on her head!"

"That's right. She hadn't worn it at the main house earlier, either, Doc. She must have put it on after she came down to the cottage and then gone out to the barn for something—or to meet somebody."

"Good God! So whoever it is hits her hard with the twitch handle. She goes down—or maybe she doesn't go down at that moment. Maybe the guy that hit her tries to hide and she gets over her original dizziness and staggers back to the cottage . . ."

Eddie didn't like the picture, either. "Any way you look at it, it's pretty foul. There's another angle I didn't bring up. She wasn't raped. So if the criminal killed her in the cottage after he'd hit her in the barn, it may have been because she got a good look at him." He shoved his coffee cup away. "From the character of that attack, the killer's got to be a goon."

Regardless of what I thought about the Angel family's place in Anita Ferrier's death there seemed no question of the fact that her killer had been what Eddie called a goon. I needed no autopsy findings to amplify my impression of that beaten body. The man may have been bent on the destruction of the woman in front of him, but he was also hysterically eager to see her punished.

For what?

I didn't argue with Marsh. "How does Feeney treat the development?"

"He likes it just fine." Marsh fumbled with cigarettes. "Doc, the Angel family is hot stuff around those parts. A little touchy around my own beat, as far as that goes. The 'tramp wandering out of the woods' theory was in there from the first, and everybody concerned welcomes any support of the idea with cheers—notably Feeney."

"The wayfaring stranger!" No blackmail threats, no "Bolado matter," no nothing! "What do you think, Eddie?"

"Me, Doc?" He must have got his stomach back, because he reached for his coffee again, took a big swig, and beamed at me. "Well now, I'll tell you. The wayfaring stranger will do quite nicely on the face of the evidence so far at hand, as they say. I'd not like to have the assignment of proving that one of those easygoing *Cubanos* did that to his sister."

"How about Ferrier?"

"He's pretty well clear, it seems to me. I'd be surprised as hell to find he had anything to do with it."

"You've been surprised as hell before, chum. As a matter of fact, I think he's out, too—blackmail and all."

"Feeney doesn't even call it blackmail. Incidentally, we'll have to pick that note up this morning . . ."

"I'll show you. What's Feeney call it?"

"I gave it to him as best I could from memory and he called the turn on it, for my money. He said nobody could convince him that any member of that tribe would carry out a threat to disgrace any other—that it was just another example of how hard they scrapped among themselves. He called my attention to the way they acted about the servants."

"How did they act?"

"Solid, Doc. Feeney had them all out there again this morning and they insisted that the house and farm people weren't bullied—stood around and said, 'Good old Perez,' 'Loyal old Charley,' and that sort of thing. I'd hate to think how they'd act if somebody showed suspicion of one of their own!"

"Did Feeney talk at any length with Ferrier?"

"No. Ferrier is a very serious guy—and a pretty impressive citizen. He's probably number one among the people Feeney wants to eliminate."

"From what you say, I can't see how Feeney would care to make very much of my story—as you suggested he might—in your pleasant way."

"I was kidding. If I were you, I'd try to get him interested. He'll throw you out. He doesn't want to make too much of any of it, but he realizes that he's got to hear it for the record."

"Right. When shall we get the blackmail note?"

"Now, if you can. That's why I'm here. Ferrier has left word for the apartment people to let us in for a routine look around."

"Has anybody talked to him about the note?"

"Not yet. I thought you might like to." He grinned mightily.

"Your academic interest is taking a new turn, Commissioner. I'd be thoroughly delighted to talk with him."

"Maybe before Feeney does, right?"

"Right!" I said it with some feeling, and we set off for the Ferrier apartment. The manager looked at Eddie's shield and let us in. There was no one in the apartment, although the place had apparently been cleaned very recently. When the manager had gone downstairs—at Eddie's polite request—I went through the bedrooms. They were in complete order.

"Did Ferrier stay at Cielito last night, Eddie?"

"No. At least I don't think so. Is it important?"

"I guess not. If he stayed here, the servants must have swamped out fast and left."

Eddie frowned. "All right. So he stayed at the Ritz. Where he was night before last might be important. Let's get that note."

We went to the library and I checked the book. Then I checked the books on each side of it. Then, for almost an hour, we checked every damned book in the place. No go.

Marsh looked at his dusty hands. "Who got it?"

"Anita Ferrier, obviously." Who else? She hid it. So I said, "Who else?"

"Ferrier."

"No. Unless he saw her hide it—which, with a person as bright as his wife was, is silly."

Eddie shook his head. "I guess I've been silly, myself. I told Feeney about the note, of course, early this morning. Ferrier didn't get there for at least an hour. I'll give you even money the first thing Feeney did when I walked out of there was to call the guy up and tell him."

"Could be—taking Feeney's attitude into consideration." Jack Ferrier would definitely protect his threatening brother-in-law as long as possible. "The woman could have taken it with her, though. You might find it around the cottage."

"There isn't anything in that place that hasn't been gone over, one way or the other. They weren't looking for a note, of course." Eddie got off his haunches and looked around for a probable bathroom door. "You'd better take it up with Ferrier. I've got a notion he'd tell you about it where he'd clam up on Feeney or me. Let's wash and get going."

When I got back to my place, I called Jack Ferrier at Cielito and told him that his wife had said some things to me that I thought should be discussed between us. He wanted to know, at once, what they were, and I assured him that I had no desire to be mysterious but that I couldn't very well discuss them under the circumstances. Cielito is on three trunks, I found from the book, later, and undoubtedly littered with extensions.

He promised to drive in soon—and arrived shortly after two. Clinic was over and I'd been staring idly out the window and saw him walking up from Eighth Avenue, where he'd probably left his car in a parking lot. When the elevator clanked up, I went to the hall door to meet him. We shook hands and simply muttered whatever salutations seemed necessary. He looked pretty droopy as we walked into the living room and I was sorry for him.

"How about a drink?"

"Yes. Thank you. I think I'd like a drink."

"Good. There are cigarettes on the end table . . ."

When I came in with the tray, he was dumped back into the couch looking rather vaguely at my horse pictures. "You like hunters."

"All my life." I set the stuff down. "This, by the way, is horsemen's whisky. I don't stock scotch."

He looked at the label. "We have whiskies in common as well as horses, Doctor."

I poured us each a substantial portion of the Old Forester and we settled down. I think we both felt that it might turn into quite a session. I opened . . .

"Let's get a couple of things straight before we go too far into the matter at hand—" Ferrier shook the ice in his drink and looked at it as he spoke, interrupting me gently.

"The matter at hand being something my wife confided to you night before last?"

"Yes." He seemed unwilling to leave the subject, so I waited.

"I wish to know one thing before we—get this couple of things of yours straight. Did what she told you have to do with any danger to her? Her—person?"

"Definitely not. Naturally, I should have taken some action at the time—you will understand that."

Ferrier put down his glass. "Of course. That's all I wanted to know, Doc. It would have made a difference."

I took up where I'd left off. "There are two things I want you to understand. First, I am neither a professional investigator nor a stool pigeon for the police. Second, because I feel a tremendous personal obligation to your late wife, I intend to investigate the circumstances of her death and report what I find to the proper authorities. Is that clear?"

"Perfectly." Ferrier relaxed—sank back deeper into the couch. "Is there any special reason why you warn me, Doctor?"

"Yes. Mrs. Ferrier told me that one of her brothers was attempting to blackmail you." I pulled back from that lighted fuse and held my ears.

The man dropped his head a moment in thought—looked up quite brightly. "That's remarkably interesting. How did she justify such an idea?"

"Pretty solidly, I'm afraid. She showed me the note you received."

"The note *I* received?" I couldn't make out what sort of emotion keyed his query. Maybe curiosity—maybe cautious restraint. But there was something there. "She *showed* you a note?

I didn't like the way it was going. "She showed me a note that had been hidden under the paper lining of your desk drawer. Shall we stop kidding each other, Ferrier?"

"You're going to be very difficult. What if I told you I had never received such a note?"

"I'm afraid I wouldn't believe you."

Ferrier made a gesture of resignation with his hands. "Before we get through here, Doc, somebody's going to have to believe somebody else. What did the note say?"

I quoted it as nearly as I could without digging for my book. It seemed a silly procedure, but if Ferrier wanted to play games I had to go along—part of the way, at least. The man acted naturally curious—nothing more. I had a quick idea that I shouldn't play poker with him. I said, "You seem curious, at least."

"I *am* curious. Very." He picked up his glass again and carefully observed how much ice had melted since he had put it down. "I'm curious to know why my wife should have thought one of her brothers had sent that note to me. I'm sure she must have known better . . ."

"It has the brother-in-law angle. It could hardly be anyone else. Have you any other brothers-in-law?"

"None." He managed a smile. Then he turned deadly serious. "Doc, how far would this sense of obligation you feel toward Anita carry you?"

I reviewed his question pretty cautiously before I dared answer. "Hell! I don't know, Jack. I can't see how I could have felt any more terribly about—someone I hadn't known before. Why?"

Ferrier compressed his lips and shook his head. "Because I'm about to trust you. I am not the trusting sort. My experience has given me little reason to believe I should . . ."

"Take it easy. Maybe you'd better think it over. I'm not anxious to incur any further feeling of obligation and there are—some kinds of confidences I'd rather not have, if you know what I mean."

He came out with a gruff, mirthless laugh. "What I have to tell you may stretch your credulity, Doc, but the confidence won't stretch your principles." His broad hand brushed over his gray hair. "All right. You suggested we stop kidding each other. I have stopped—as of now."

"Do we start over the situation again—or can we go on from where we were?" I found myself wanting to believe the guy, for some reason.

"We go on. I did a little stalling on the subject of the note because I—"

"Excuse me. You did know about it, then?"

"Yes. I knew about it," The gray man sighed deeply. "You see, when you told me, just now, about Anita's finding the note, I couldn't see why she hadn't explained something of its significance to you."

"I don't believe she saw any significance, Jack. She said she had no idea what it was all about."

Ferrier stared at the floor for some time. Looked up. "It's possible, of course . . ." Then he trailed off into his thoughts again.

I waited for him to say something—then asked, "When did you receive the note?"

He was slow in answering, kept studying the rug. "Doc, I've puzzled over what we're calling the 'Bolado matter' for a number of years. It has been—dormant. Circumstances—the kind of bitter disagreements which the family has been having—have created a favorable atmosphere for its being brought back." Ferrier stood up and wandered over to the hearth, stood with his neat back to me as he seemed to study a jumping picture. When he was ready, he turned with a sort of resoluteness in his manner. "You see, Doc, I wrote that letter myself."

"To one of your brothers-in-law?"

Ferrier smiled with some inner irony—a wry, bitter smile. "Yes. To one of my brothers-in-law. It was never sent."

"May I ask why?"

"Certainly. I never knew which one to send it to."

7

STILL THURSDAY EVENING, OCTOBER 4

It's late and I'm pretty well bushed, but the "Bolado matter" has me by the throat and I've got to set it down. My talk with Jack Ferrier went through several hours—went through, also, a substantial portion of the Forester decanter and the Angel family closet, where hangs a skeleton of considerable stature.

It is not, as such skeletons are apt to be, that of a minor deed, like the embezzlement of entrusted funds or spoliation of the entrusted honor of some transient maid, a type of thievery more to be expected of the mettlesome Angels. Unhappily it is neither.

It is the small and rather pathetic skeleton of a thirteen-year-old boy who—after being washed up on a rough Cuban beach—was identified as one Caesar Bolado Vega.

For reasons of his own, the boy called himself simply Bolado and was known as such to the watermen for whom he occasionally ran errands and from whom he occasionally begged rides to the fishing grounds and even to Miami, itself.

But the story of little Bolado is Jack Ferrier's story, of course, and he should tell it. Many of the words in my notebook, here, are his. I'll set it down for you much as he told it—interrupting this tale as little as I did his narrative this afternoon, when he sat there with his replenished drink and tinkled the ice again.

"It goes a long way back, Doc—and from the day I decided what the truth about the affair must have been, I've never discussed it with anybody. Not even my wife. But I hadn't forgotten it. It's the sort of thing that crawls into your brain and lays its eggs there. But I had learned to put it aside. That wasn't easy because, you see, it concerns somebody with whom I am associated every day—part of my very family—a brother of my wife . . .

"About eight weeks ago, a man came to me and announced that he had all the facts of the Bolado affair—and, of course, that they were for sale. I bought them." Ferrier lit a cigarette and waited for my question. When I didn't ask it, he said, "I bought them for a great deal more money than I can afford to pay for anything."

Then I asked the one he didn't expect. "Was it a man called Buzz Chapin?"

It shook him. The man was violently startled. I should have waited. He looked at me in a puzzled, apprehensive way. "I don't like that, Doc. I think I've made a pretty bad mistake."

"Because I happened to guess who it was?"

Then he had control of himself—his eyes cold. "Guess? Out of several million people you *guess,* Connor? You'll have to do better than that!"

I did better than that for some fifteen or twenty minutes. It had been somewhat as Truck Snowden had said. Chapin had hung around the Angel family off and on for several years, both in Havana during their last two winters there and in New York. Neither Ferrier nor I could make any sense at all out of the husband-enraging remark. Ferrier, finally satisfied, went on.

"Chapin's documents contained nothing more than I already knew. The important thing is that, to my knowledge, there wasn't another soul in the world, including four of the Angel brothers—and, of course, excepting one—who had even an inkling of the Bolado affair."

I couldn't help asking where Chapin had got his information.

"I don't know. He wouldn't tell me—and the fact that he had it was enough. I couldn't, for my wife's sake, permit anyone to have that information."

"Blackmail is nasty business, Jack. I'm afraid he'll be back."

"No," his voice was carefully subdued, "he won't be back.

The payment of a large sum for blackmail is also nasty business, Doc. When Chapin brought me the stuff, I made him a very simple and understandable proposition."

"Oh? I didn't know you could do that with blackmailers."

"You can with this one. He signed a receipt for the papers, stating that he had sold them in full understanding that the transaction was blackmail. Then I told him that, if the information ever became public through any source except those specific documents, I'd kill him."

Ferrier turned away and sipped his drink. Then he smiled a little and said, "Chapin understood that."

"I can understand it, too." I would have believed him if he'd said it to me.

"Suppose we go back some twenty-two years, Doc, and see why the Bolado matter could be so damaging. Why I almost broke myself paying for Chapin's documents and why I was so sorely tempted to charge the bill where it belonged—to the man I'd been forced to protect for Nita's sake.

"I was . . ." He found the answer on the ceiling. "I was thirty-two years old and broke. The 1929 thing had set me back from a very decent spot in a brokerage office in New York to a wildcat sugar and banana peddler out of Miami. I got through the crash with a few thousand dollars. The break came in October and by December I was out walking the streets with a lot of good training in a business nobody ever wanted to hear of again—and nothing else.

"I knew only two other things reasonably well—horses and power boats—neither of which was calculated to make me much of a living. It got sleety in New York and I figured what the hell and headed for Florida. There, of course, I wasn't very long learning that, in 1930, the boys around Miami had found a very profitable use for power-boating experience. But I learned another thing, too.

"I learned that the small dockside banana operators were screaming for bananas and that the bootleggers were screaming for sugar that could be bought on sight and unseen. In those days every bottom that would float was staggering across the Havana-Miami chop with whisky. The only bananas they bought around the islands were strictly props.

"So I picked up an old hull, worked it over a little, and got on the run—but legitimate. It wasn't too bad."

Ferrier grinned to himself, shook his head, and sipped his drink. "In kicking around Havana, I first met the Angel family. The six of them—I met the boys first—were all within ten years of the same age. They ranged, then, from fifteen to twenty-five or so and were the life of the town in one way or another. I met Carlos and Johnny first, I think. They are next to the oldest. Ramon's the oldest. Anyway, the three of us had a good time around town and, later, did some game fishing together in the boat. Lonny and Merry—I suppose you have them in that notebook of yours as Alonso and Mariano—Lonny and the kid went along on some of those fishing trips.

"They were a pretty nice bunch, Doc. Wild as hares in a pleasant sort of way—American-educated and a swell combination of warm temperament and *yanqui* enthusiasm. They liked me, too, and one Sunday they took me home with them to meet their sister. Well—that did it, Doc. She was—oh well, you know—don't you?"

"I know, Jack."

There were a couple of things said at this point which I can neither remember—nor wish to. I think we had another drink. I know we made corned-beef sandwiches in the kitchen. I felt glad that he had the Bolado problem to worry about—no matter what it cost him. Provided, always, that it had not cost Anita's life.

When we'd settled again, he said, "There was a kid around the docks at that time called Bolado. He was thirteen—although I would have guessed him a year or so older at the time. The boy would run errands, swab a deck for a private owner, row in and out with groceries and ice—that sort of thing. I learned—later, of course—that his father was a widower and a notorious wino who would disappear for a week at a time. Apparently not another soul had any interest in the kid whatever. I put this in now, although I didn't know it at that time, because it accounts for the fact that nobody knew anything about him along the water front and that only strangers would ask him why he didn't go home instead of sleeping a week at a time in the corner of some *depósito*.

"So, when he disappeared from his haunts one day, nobody missed him. If anybody had hollered for him to haul some groceries or ice, it would have been a matter of inconvenience rather than concern that the boy had probably bummed his way to Miami again—to stand there on the dock and admire the *Americanos*, whom he worshiped.

"Then, when his body—or what the barracuda and crabs had left of it—was washed up on the beach, everybody said, 'Too damn bad,' and 'Somebody should have taken better care of him. He was a nice kid.' And that was the end of it.

"That was the end of it, Doc, for everybody but me. I knew what had happened to him. I didn't know right then—I wasn't sure, I mean, while the perfunctory police examination was being made. I didn't know until I'd exhausted every possible angle I could dig up to make it an accident.

"Doc, one of the five Angel boys killed him."

I intruded here. "I suppose it wouldn't do any good to ask which one again—"

"It wouldn't, because I don't know. It was simple enough. All the brothers had learned how to run the old tub and any two of them could handle her. Actually, I'd handled her alone many times—although she usually required some nursing along below at the times somebody had to be on the bridge. I say this because it's possible that on the day young Bolado disappeared, one man did operate the boat—at least part of the time.

"A major point is that, being an irregular buyer of stuff for the States, I had to wait around sometimes for a deal. After I got to know the Angel family so well, I hauled a moorage up the beach and dumped it where I could tie up in a nicer place whenever I wanted during those waits.

"We'd run out from there and fish or bat along around the point and have a feed—that sort of thing. My one-man crew was glad enough to get away at those times. He had a girl around town somewhere and didn't bother to use his bunk aboard.

"So I used to leave a set of cabin and ignition keys at the Angel house. Anita was twenty-six, then—and mothered the brood. Their father was in the States most of the time and their mother was dead. I suppose she'd have married . . ." Ferrier put his glass down. "Goddammit! Let's get on with this!" The business of a cigarette filled the break.

"On the day in question, I was working on a deal in town. I got back about six and went straight to the Angels', where I hung around and had dinner. Nothing seemed wrong. All the boys were home when I got there. I didn't have any reason to look for the keys in the hall-table drawer, of course, but I have no doubt they were there at the time.

"After dinner we had some coffee outside and the kids, Lonny and Merry, went off to a show or something. It was all perfectly normal. We had done the same thing often . . .

"I went back to the beach about nine and rowed out to the boat. I didn't notice anything unusual about the tender. It was in its regular spot and the oars carefully padlocked as we always left them. When I got to the boat, I went directly to my bunk, read awhile, and slept.

"In the morning my engineer walked up the beach and hollered out to the moorage for me to get him aboard—that there was a load of stuff for us at the dock. I rowed in and got him and we shoved off. He was below when I went up for the first time that morning, to the bridge deck—it was one of those freak gimmicks you see in those waters, awkwardly high and aft of the cabin hatch. I noticed immediately that someone had been using the boat—or, at least, fooling around with the controls.

"I yelled down to see if my engineer had been aboard yesterday. He said no, but somebody had left the gaff dirty and if it was me I'd better trade places with him. I figured the Angel boys had been fishing and didn't think much about it. I made a mental note, though, to give one of them hell for leaving the binnacle light on. Or for turning it on in the full glare of the

Cuban sun. It couldn't be knocked on or off accidentally. I had installed it myself and put the tumbler switch under the case.

"Even Merry, who was a timid sort of kid, wouldn't have played around with that switch. It annoyed me.

"In twenty minutes we were docking and I was greeted by an also annoyed gent who wanted to know where the hell we'd been and did we want his business or didn't we? From then on until we set out for Miami I was busy with clearance, some needed supplies, fuel, and a quick call to Anita to say good-by for a while. My 'By the way, did the kids go aboard the boat yesterday?' drew only a casual negative.

"When we were well warmed up and away, I turned the bridge over to the engineer and went below—mildly curious about the dirty gaff. Nothing that could be hooked ordinarily at the moorage would call for a gaff. That would mean that the boys had taken her out into the deep water. Even if they'd fished from the moorage, they must have had the key, because the gaff was inside the locked main hatch.

"Charley, the engineer, had laid the gaff on some shelving above the engine. I asked him where he found it and he said it had fallen alongside the crankcase through a space in the decking of the engine room. Its place was on the cockpit bulkhead, held there by a couple of metal clips. Obviously, it is for use there where the fish can be gaffed or clubbed as they are hauled inboard from the water.

"The gaff was badly messed with blood and, at the moment, I was sore at the kids because we'd always had rules about the gear—and they had been good about keeping them. I washed the gaff overside and put it away.

"That was the start, Doc. I looked into the fish boxes and they were clean. I looked at the tackle and it was in perfect order. Then, for some reason which I can't explain to you, I unreeled some line on every rig, big and small, aboard. There was no damp line.

"Later, while were tied up in Miami, I found what, then, seemed to be a simple answer to my mystery of the burning binnacle light. I found the dirty old officer's cap I'd given Bolado, the kid. It was under the little anchor decking of the tender—a sort of stow hole where we shoved odds and ends we wanted to keep dry. The boy had probably rowed out with one of the Angels, caught a fish at the moorage, and killed it as though it had been a big one, with the gaff handle." He paused.

My hair began to prickle in my scalp. I couldn't help whispering, "The gaff *handle?*"

There was a terrible and desperate look in Ferrier's eyes. They begged. "Please, Doc—wait a minute, will you? Let me finish!"

"I'm sorry . . ."

"That's what I thought *then,* Doc. That the boy had killed a fish. That's what I thought until I got back to Havana and learned—quite casually—that Bolado had been washed up. That he was chewed almost beyond identification. That the squall we'd slobbered through on the way back had not only washed him ashore but had fractured his skull and hammered him against the rocks.

"I don't think I'd do it again, but what difference does that make now? I hid the cap for a while—then I dropped it overside far out. I got rid of it when I found that all five of the boys had been on separate errands of one sort or another that afternoon—and when Anita told me she had been home all afternoon and nobody had taken the keys from the drawer.

"One of them *had* taken the keys that day, Doc. Nita and I were married a few months later. I have never, in all our wonderfully happy life together, mentioned the subject to her."

I went into the kitchen, turned the water on full blast, banged ice trays around, and raised hell generally. I figured that anything was better, just at that moment, than to tell him that the documents which had caused him so much concern—and cost him so much money—were probably once again in the wrong hands.

8

This morning I had a session with Feeney, who pretended he'd come to the city to see me. I would have been flattered, perhaps, if Eddie Marsh hadn't called me first and said the guy had been wheedling around downtown trying to find out if anybody would try to make him look bad if he just kept on hunting for wayfaring strangers.

Eddie had simply played dumb and sent him on to me.

I gave him just what he'd already heard and no more. Following Marsh's advice, I tried to make a mystery out of the note—excluding my intruder, which I considered my business for the moment—and sell it to him. He gave me the wise yeah-yeah-yeah—then the no-no-couldn't-be . . .

"Not with this kind of people, Doc. It won't button up. They'll send each other notes and holler and yell, but they just plain don't beat people to death with clubs." All this with a patronizing, smile to make it nice. "Besides, there ain't one whit of physical evidence that gets anywhere near anybody on the Angel place."

With this, and some few other choice observations, he left. I asked him if he'd want to see me again, soon, as he waited for the elevator. He just looked at me with that big, stupid grin and said, "Why, Doc?"

As they say on the panel programs, that's a very good question. At any rate, for the time being at least, I'm sprung from the clutches of the Tioga Village law.

About eleven-thirty, I decided the newly wealthy Mr. Chap-in would be studying the racing papers in a sixty-dollar bath-robe and it was time to chat with him. His address was right in the telephone book like anybody else's, so I hacked over. When I got to the door of his very modern apartment, he called for me to come on in.

I was wrong. He was wearing a ninety-dollar dressing gown and was reading the *Mirror*.

"Hello, Doc! Come in. There's some coffee still hot in the kitchen."

My pal! I dropped my hat and sat down. "Thanks. I stopped by to find out what you meant by your crack about my judo practice."

"Oh?" He managed to look quite happy about it. "You aren't getting sensitive to that sort of thing, are you?"

"I'm afraid I am. Let's have it!"

He tossed the paper over to a table and got up—went out into the kitchen. "Sure you won't join me in a cup of coffee?"

"Quite sure—thanks." My temper isn't any too good under some conditions. I had to restrain myself from telling him what a louse I knew he was—and backing it up.

He came in with his coffee. "Sure, I'll tell you, Doc. There isn't any secret about it. The only thing is that, since I needled you about it, the thing got to be no joke any more. I can't say I blame you for being—let's call it intense—about it."

"All right, what was a joke the other day—and isn't now?"

"The fact that Anita Ferrier was making a play for you. It seemed amusing at the time."

I checked a number of things I wanted to say. "Where did you get that idea?"

"Oh—around, Doc." He drank coffee smugly.

"Has anybody from homicide been to see you yet, by the way?"

The guy stopped drinking his coffee fast. *"Homicide!* Why would they want to see me? My God! You don't think I go 'round killing beautiful women, do you?"

"Frankly, I don't know, Buzz—unless one of them had robbed you of a beautiful man . . ."

"You—bastard!" He was really goosed by that one. But I wanted him hotter than a Yuma rock. "Why did you come here, anyway?"

"I came here to find out what you know about the Ferriers and the Angel family—any of 'em and all of 'em!" I stood up and took a step toward him. It was strictly B-picture, but escaped Chapin's critical faculties for the moment.

"Wait a minute, Doc! I hardly know them to speak to—"

"Nuts! Havana the last two winters—Cielito—the races. Don't sit there and lie to me. How did you know Anita Ferrier was going to get in touch with me?"

"What do you mean was going to? Now who's lying? Homicide men coming to see *me!* Why, goddammit, Anita Ferrier was in your apartment last Friday night for hours! It's none of my business what you—"

I hollered, then. "How do you know? How do you know she was in my apartment last Friday night?"

"Oh! So now, you—"

"Shut up! *Shut up* and listen to me!" I advanced on him some more, if I remember correctly, and it was real enough, this time, to make him get out of his chair and scurry half across the room. I stalked after him. "How do you know she was there Friday night?"

"Because I saw her go in." I think he improvised from there on. Maybe not. "I was standing on the corner of Forty-eighth and Broadway about eight forty-five and saw her go into your building. I was curious and waited. Then you—or she—pulled the shades down. I went on to the Garden."

"Was she alone? When she went in, I mean?"

"Yes. As if you didn't know."

"You didn't see a man go in—either with her or very nearly the same time—maybe a man smoking a cigar?"

"No." He calmed a little—looked puzzled. "Why the man with the cigar?"

"Because there had to be a man with a cigar with her—if she was there at all."

"Sounds crazy as hell."

"It is crazy as hell. I wasn't there. I was at the fights, too. They left a cigar odor behind them. I want to know who the man was."

"Maybe you don't know Anita Ferrier as well as I thought . . ." He grinned a peace offering—of which I wanted no part, but didn't growl. "Were you around her enough to notice what she smokes?"

"What *she* smokes? Why—no. The only time I was ever with her to speak to, she was having cocktails. She—"

"Never smoked when she drank anything. That right?"

"That's what she told me. Why?"

"When she did smoke—which was absolutely incessantly when she wasn't drinking—she smoked those foul Cuban cigarettes. They're made of cigar tobacco, you know . . ."

I did some mental staggering around under that, but kept on talking. "I didn't find any butts around—but then that wouldn't mean anything."

"If you had, it wouldn't have been Nita. She doesn't leave things around."

"Tidy, eh?"

"Very."

There was nothing else in him I could get—and he annoyed me for ten minutes trying to find out why Anita Ferrier had been in my apartment while I was at the fights. I got out and went home with plenty to think about.

What was it with her that she calmly spent hours searching a strange man's apartment? Desperation I'd understand—but that would be tense, hurried—pressing. She'd hardly have wandered around the place with a cigarette in her mouth. On the other hand, she was the type of completely confident woman who could have turned her criminal entry into a sort of a fellow conspiracy with me in five minutes . . .

"It is quite simple, Doctor Connor. It is true that I have been searching your apartment—but what I am searching for concerns me, not you. If you are holding it here, I assure you that you are more at fault than I. Please give it to me." I could imagine the switch she'd make at that point—from stern reason to fine scorn. "Or, if you prefer, *sell* it to me."

It would have been just that easy. I'd have told her I didn't have what she wanted, convinced her of it, and we'd have been off on a treasure hunt. The woman I'd talked to the night before her death would have had the courage—and the imagination—to make such a plan and get away with it. Actually, she was taking no chances of serious embarrassment.

I needed to see Jack Ferrier again. The fact that his wife had been so deeply concerned would, perhaps, give him a new light on her knowledge of the Bolado affair.

I called Ferrier and suggested he come over.

When he arrived, he was extremely nervous and pretty much exhausted. He'd apparently held up about as long as he could take it. I didn't offer him a drink, but dragged him into the office and gave him some mild sedation—insisted he sit around a few minutes. After a while he shook his head and dug for a cigarette. "That helped a lot, Doc—thanks."

"You can't do it all at once, Jack. Take it easy. Let's go back where it's a little less professional." We went through to the living room. "Sit down and get comfortable. I've got some new information to give you—and a couple of questions to ask. Are you up to it?"

"Of course. It's got to get worse before it gets better." He squeezed his eyes closed, opened them, and grinned punchily. "Go ahead."

"Jack, your wife must have recognized the name Bolado in the letter she found. Right?"

"She should have—though it may have been without any particular significance. She would remember the boy's death, of course."

"But you have never discussed it between you?"

He smiled gently. "No, Doc, never. Even if it had had some unpleasant connotation to her, we'd not have discussed it—unless she wanted it discussed. Perhaps our—relationship was unusual—"

"Unusual, perhaps, I'd say, but certainly sound."

"Tell me again—maybe exactly, if you can remember—what she said about the name." He knuckled his hair fiercely. "I keep getting the feeling I could call her up and ask!"

"Of course." I thought it over carefully. "I believe she said that she knew of no way in which the name Bolado could be used as a threat against you. Would that have meant that she might have known that it could have been used as a threat against someone else? Does that sound like an evasion she might make?"

"I suppose so—under great pressure. She wasn't given to evasion." Ferrier gathered himself together as though for a jump. "Look, Doc; I've got something on my mind I've got to know about before we go any further. I've put it off because—well, I suppose it's because I thought you'd say something about it. Or—perhaps . . ." He bogged down.

"Tell me."

"Did you ever receive an envelope through the mail from me?"

"From *you?*"

"Yes. From me. There was one envelope inside another—the outer one plain, the inner one sealed, but with a note asking you if you would be kind enough to hold it safely for a few days."

"Was it signed by you—the inside note?"

"Yes." He stared impatiently at me. "I asked particularly that it not be opened."

"I got such an envelope, Jack—at least it was delivered here—and I didn't open it." I collected my courage and jumped in. "Unfortunately, the letter was stolen from me—from the apartment."

I explained that it had been taken before I'd read the note and expected nothing less than fireworks, but he just sat there and grinned. "That's too bad, Doc."

"You don't seem too perturbed—what's funny about it?"

"When was it stolen?"

"Late Tuesday afternoon—or during the evening. I was away at the races until time to go to your place for cocktails—then had dinner with Katie Storm after that." It occurred to me for the first time that Anita Ferrier knew Katie and I were dining— that she could have come back for a last try. I explained to him about the previous attempts to find the letter. "I'm still curious to know why you don't think it's very important, Jack."

"All right. Perhaps I'd better clarify it in some detail. Did you suspect what had been in the inner envelope, Doc?"

"I had pretty good reason to. There was a correction slip—a flimsy from a carbon copy, apparently—left in the outer envelope. It had the name Bolado on it."

Ferrier smiled quietly again. "That's right. I faked it, Doc. The thing was bait. Sorry to have planted it on you—but you seemed a most likely sort of person. It didn't work out just as I had expected. I had hoped someone would make overtures to you—certainly not rob your apartment. You see, Doc, I thought I had it all planned out." The man leaned back in the couch and stared at the ceiling.

"In the first place, you must remember that we were dealing with an incident of long ago—twenty years ago. It had been ticketed as an accident by the police and certainly wouldn't have been reinvestigated because of some gossip. There would be nothing to find. As a result, I had no reason to think that anything could result from it but a very nasty piece of public gossip. I felt that I, being the only one who knew the truth—or part of the truth, at least—of the affair, should do what I could to check it.

"I paid Chapin off with full intentions of taking it out of his hide later—and with equally full intentions of smoking out the right member of the family to reimburse me if I couldn't get my money back from Chapin someway."

"So you set a trap for him."

"That's right, Doc."

"All for your wife's sake, of course."

"Of course. Why would I care a damn about the rest of them?"

"And now it doesn't make any difference what happens. That right, Jack?"

"That's exactly right. All I want now is to get my hands on that rotten degenerate and kill him." He tensed and flexed his hands.

I hurried him off the subject. "How did you bait this trap—how'd you work it?"

"I went around muttering about some rather touchy family documents and said I didn't want the responsibility of keeping them—in the hope one of the brothers would insist on accepting that responsibility. Nothing happened. They did ask me what they were about and I played cagey. Then I let it be known that I was going to look you up—that I'd heard you were sort of a high-class detective. All this was spread over a period of some time. I even called Truck Snowden in front of some of the others."

"Was Mrs. Ferrier—Anita—in on this?"

"If you mean in on the plot, no. She knew what was going on, naturally, through her brothers."

"So then you mailed the letter?"

"That's right." He studied a moment. "I mailed it on Thursday—the day before you say somebody broke in here the first time. I certainly wish I'd known about it."

"I wish you had, too, Jack. I hate like hell to tell you, but I've just found out that the person who's been searching this place—and the one who most probably got the envelope on Tuesday night—was your wife."

He must have rejected several of the things he started to say. He froze to the couch—erect—taut. Then he let out his breath and said, very quietly, "What makes you think that, Doc?"

"She was seen coming in here that Friday evening—the first time."

"That's certain?"

"It couldn't be any other way." The guy was sagging and I felt rotten about it, but, as he had said, it had to get worse before it got better. "If either of us had known more about it, Jack, we could have done something. Don't blame yourself. Maybe we'd better think about the Bolado papers and where they may have got to—or did you mail the actual documents?"

"That's the heartbreaking part of it, Doc! The nasty, miserable irony of it. The Bolado documents are in my safe at the office and my wife—my loyal, wonderful Anita—gave her life for an envelope full of old newspaper!"

Later, as I watched the elevator disappear below, I stood in the doorway and thought, bitterly, of the fact that Anita Ferrier had died distrusting me. She must have gone directly from our meeting to my apartment—to find the envelope square in the middle of my desk. The envelope I had failed to mention to her because I hadn't known it existed!

Somewhere, all along the way, the timing has been off.

9

But that, of course, was yesterday.

Tonight I'm in Havana. Now that I'm here, I can't exactly figure out why—except that I remember agreeing with Jack Ferrier last night, while my circulatory system was distributing seven ounces of Old Forester, that all the answers would be here. By now my bonded boldness has gone its expensive and devious ways and I am sitting in my shorts under a lazy ceiling fan.

From the payed jungle below my windows come a thousand rumba bands in a thousand stages of attenuation. From somewhere near, a very loud and very bad singer roars his Latin rhythms against the savage crash-and-bell of an American cash register. It's all richly native—with most of the natives from Georgia and Alabama this time of year. It seems that most of the local people whose presence is required in the city during the day flee the night hours and crouch until morning in some very handsome retreats out of sight and sound of the invading Americans.

One such retreat is Cielo, the plantation of the Angel family. I am assured that *Cielo* means heaven by no less an authority than the University of Chicago's Spanish Dictionary, which I bought this morning at La Guardia Airport for thirty-five cents. *Cielito,* among other things, means little heaven—no matter how vast it may seem out there on Long Island. Thus, I mastered the language on my flight, between naps.

Incidentally, I may have sold my soul for the passage and my expenses here. Jack Ferrier is picking up the tab. It's the first reimbursement I've received for any of my cops-'n'-robbers activities and I feel a bit silly about it.

My purpose here is simple in definition—probably extremely complex in accomplishment. I am in Havana to locate the person from whom Buzz Chapin got his information—and his affidavits. Jack Ferrier seems convinced that, whoever that person may be, he will know which of the brothers Angel went aboard the boat that day in the autumn of 1931. Chapin's source could have reserved that as an ace in the hole—after having given him sufficient for blackmailing purposes. The family, after all, was a richer unit than the individual. Between them, Anita and Jack Ferrier possessed most of all.

There is no other way I can get at Chapin—or the killer. Little by little, I am building up a picture of him—the killer. Not the palpable, physical exterior, of course, but the real culprit nonetheless. He has lurked, sulking and brooding, within the restricting confines of a strongly disciplined personality —one which, frightened by his first vicious emergence more than twenty years ago, must have policed him well. Until last Wednesday morning.

"Little Willie killed his sister . . ."

The old jingle has recurred so frequently to me that I think of the murderer in those terms. The basis is sound. The physical body in which Willie has so long resided is between thirty-seven and forty-seven years old. Little Willie, himself, as described in the rhyme, is about six. He will have gained strength, craftiness, and, perhaps, some small measure of sullen restraint. But he will not have learned to accept defeat or humiliation if either of these common human experiences happens to fall into a pattern relating to his six-year-old world.

I know that I shall be able to find Willie only by recreating a set of circumstances approximating those which had triggered his furious appearances before. Only young Bolado and Anita Ferrier knew, before they died, what these circumstances would be. Perhaps there is someone here in Havana who will know.

This evening, earlier, I changed into some lightweight clothing and nosed around the town. It was getting cooler and a promising breeze was coming in off the water. Early in my travels I ran into a former Miami bartender I'd known, barside, on my occasional visits there. Among other things, he told me that his former boss, Bert Lillio, was head-waiting at a place up the street called El Carib. I'd had some laughs with Bert and decided he'd be a good guy to ask some innocent questions. Lillio would be the perfect man to know that I was in Havana absorbing some color for a book—having, to my knowledge, read one of mine once.

He greeted me at the bar with a beautiful, professional bow and "What the hell are you doing in Havana in October?"

"Quiet! I'm incognito."

"Is that good?"

"Better when people don't know you're a writer. How about a seat in a corner someplace? I may want to ask you a question or two when you get a minute."

"What can I lose? I haven't seen you since you went out of Miami, one night, with a horse." We headed for the rear of the room. "That was like a year ago, wasn't it?"

"More like two, Bert. Your card said you'd read the book I got out of that."

"Yeah. I get a lot of time to read around here in the summer."

"How long you been in Havana this trip?" We came to an empty table. "This all right?"

"Sure. If it's far enough back for you. I been here four months, Doc, since the last of May."

I sat down and Bert handed me a menu—waved for the waiter. "Ever run into a guy by the name of Chapin, Bert? Buzz Chapin?"

"What's he do?" He looked toward the front, spotted a party at the hat-check desk.

"He's a hustler—a mark-up man. Goes for the fast buck."

"Never heard of him. There's a guy in the place who has, though—if my guess is any good. Want me to send him around."

"Sure. That'd be fine. Can I trust the guy?"

"No." Then Bert was off to the front. The waiter came and
I ordered a planter's punch—made with Old Forester. The man
gave it a take, looked sadly at me, and went his way. Americans in Havana—or Paris—order stuff like ice cream and brown
gravy if they like it that way.

After I'd fooled around waiting for the drink awhile, I saw a
man ploughing across to my table. His expression suggested he
was about to sell me some French post cards. He was Chinese—
at least his parents had been. He talked like Atlantic Avenue
in Brooklyn with a touch of San Francisco's chronic laryngitis.

"Bert Lillio said you were looking for me."

"I was looking for somebody who might know a man called
Chapin."

He sat down. "Buzz Chapin—a New York guy?"

"That's right. Have a drink?" The waiter put down my
planter's punch and looked expectantly—if distastefully—at my
guest.

"I'll have a double gin on the rocks with a dash of bitters."
His clothes were good enough and he was clean. The leer which
had suggested the post cards persisted. The waiter went away.
"I know Chapin, mister."

"Good. How well?"

He looked around the room. "Oh—so-so. He asked questions,
I answered them. That's how I know most people around here."

"I see." That was the way he was going to know me, too.
"Do you remember Chapin's being in Havana two, three months
ago? Bert seemed to think you might."

He sipped his drink. Grinned at me with the leer off. Then
he lit a cigarette and grinned again. "I'll tell you, friend, I'm
strictly a pro. I'm the complete local information bureau—for
the groceries."

"O.K., how much? If I need it that badly, I'll buy it."

"Twenty dollars, American—if you don't want the guy's life
history."

"That's fair. You got his life history, too?"

He gave me that bland grin again. "I can get it."

"How long you been around Havana?"

"Five years steady, now. That's long enough to know quite a lot of things."

"Yeah." I put my wallet on my lap and dug out a twenty-dollar bill. "I might want to know quite a lot of things, at that." I folded the note and gave it to him. "Now. How about Chapin?"

"He came here like the last of July—maybe first of August. He lay pretty low and didn't do much talking around. He wanted to know some things, and a friend of mine sent him to me."

"What'd he want to know?"

"What's *that* worth to you?"

I waved the waiter up and asked for the check. "It isn't worth anything to me. He wanted to know something about the accidental death of a kid named Bolado."

The man blinked a pair of interesting, slotty eyes at me. "Yeah. That's what he was asking about."

"Do you want to do some—professional work for me?"

"Why not?" He pulled a pencil and some papers out of his coat pocket. Sat waiting.

"I want to go over the same ground Chapin went over—for a different reason."

"Ground he went over with me? Or afterward?"

"Both. Maybe especially afterward. Can you find out where he went and who he saw?"

"I think so."

The waiter finished his audit and gave me the check. I paid it and he went away. The man across the table said, "You a cop?"

"No." While I had my wallet out, I gave him another twenty. "Are you?"

"I am a *holgazán.*" He didn't offer to explain and I dismissed it, secure in my possession of the U. of C.'s splendid lexicon— *nuevo y conciso.* "I do as little as I can to earn as much money as possible. When necessary, I am able to become extremely active."

"All right. Turn on a little of that, from here in. The twenty will serve as a retainer. Then how much—like per day?" I had some thought of possible unpleasant consequences attendant to the association, but gave them up in favor of having found the man—or one of the men—I was searching. I didn't, however, stop to wonder how I had found him so easily!

"Just keep the twenties coming, mister. I'm your man." He pocketed the money. "Now, want to give me your name and tell me how I can keep in touch with you?"

"My name is Jim Connor. I'm at the Serrano. Where do you start?"

"I start at the point where Chapin left me . . ." He hesitated—drained the last of his drink. "You mind telling me just what you're after. Or just what Chapin was after?"

"I guess not. I'm a New York writer. I've made a specialty for a good many years of writing about the fast-dollar boys—the Chapins—around town. Now I'm doing a book on the lads who peddle the gossip—in the right places—if you know what I mean."

"You're giving me a low opinion of myself, but I know what you mean." This time the grin was in full phase. *"Blackmailers of the Past and Present?"*

"Like that, anyway. You're—getting a little far ahead."

"O.K. If I wasn't curious, I'd get no place as Havana's leading information service."

"Tell me one thing. Did Bert Lillio know you talked with Chapin last summer?"

At this turn, the Chinese laughed. "Trying to figure out how just the guy you wanted got here so quick, Connor?"

"Yes. That's right. How?"

"Lillio's a nice guy. He minds his own business and stays out of trouble. He likes me because I mind everybody's business but my own and still stay out of trouble. The rest of the grifters that hang around, it don't pay him to know. So he doesn't know 'em—see? But he knew Chapin looked me up. That's how it was."

"I see." I got ready to go. "Now, what's your name?"

"Fan-tan."

"Like the game?"

"That's right." He stood up. "Like the game. I've got other names, but everybody around here just calls me Fan-tan. Maybe you'd better just call me that, too."

We stopped and stood, for a moment, on the sidewalk. I said, "You speak remarkably good English."

"I also do minor calculations without the use of long sleeves. They discouraged that sort of thing at P.S. 9 in Brooklyn. How about meeting me here at maybe like nine tomorrow? I may have something."

On reference to my *diccionario, nuevo y conciso,* I find that a *holgazán* is a lazy fellow—a loafer—a hooligan.

10

In *apología,* it had been my intention—which I now recognize as not only somewhat unprincipled but completely impossible—simply to toss Spanish phrases from my *diccionario* into this narrative in a splendid, traveled way and let you infer what you wished. Complexities of the language, already apparent to me, suggest that I abandon that course. From here on, I shall try to interpret such Spanish sounds as I hear straight out of the book. Frankly, my own Spanish is limited to half a dozen things to eat, some parts of a stock saddle, a few girls' names, and the usual assortment of oaths—with the usual misunderstanding of their various intensities. Complaints by linguists should be addressed not to me, but to Pocket Books, Inc., New York, publishers of my treasured lexicon.

This morning it was raining fitfully out and looked uninviting. After I'd got comfortably into a fresh pair of shorts and was lolling around under the fan wondering about my Chinese friend, somebody rapped timidly at my door. It was a short, squat guy, beefing about two hundred pounds, all of which seemed to be going in the wrong directions. He had an extremely large felt hat in one hand and a paper of some sort in the other.

"Hexcus, *señor!* Eet hees a message."

He shoved the envelope at me. I took it, dug a buck out of the trousers I'd left hanging from a dresser drawer, and gave it to him—started to close the door. He moved a huge foot, very gently, smiled shyly, and said, "Hi am to wait, *señor*." You couldn't have closed the door with a bulldozer.

"Oh . . ." I glanced at the note in my hand. "All right. Come in and sit down."

The fellow wedged his tremendous squareness into the doorway—hesitated in some heavy confusion. I thought, at first, he might have been searching the room for a chair which wouldn't embarrass him. Then he gave a quick, agonized glance at my shorts and backed hurriedly into the hall. "Hi wait ou'side, *señor!*"

I closed the door on the maidenly monster and turned my attention to the letter.

> My dear Dr. Connor,
> A friend who keeps in touch, for professional purposes, with New York-Havana travel has informed me of your trip. For reasons which, I suspect, you will readily understand, I followed immediately. I am aware of the purpose of your visit—and, of course, of the sincerity of your intentions. I believe it would be well, however, for you to talk with me before you inevitably injure innocent people.
>   What about a drink together tomorrow afternoon? My servant will call for you at any hour you suggest.
>   Sincerely yours, Carlos Angel.

"Followed immediately" . . . for reasons I could "readily understand"! Something told me, as the feller says, that I'd see him all right—or take the next plane to New York. Cuba is a very fine place—for Cubans and peacefully intentioned visitors. But something also told me that the Angel name and all that Angel sugar could well make Havana considerably less than a tropical playground for a guy intent on destroying a prominent citizen. On a number of occasions I have been known to dash blithely into dangerous situations. In this moment of humility, I hasten to admit that, most of the time, I didn't know they were loaded.

I called the monster back—first putting on a robe in the interests of delicacy.

"Señor?"

"You have brought me a very fine invitation from the *Señor* Angel. I thank you."

He bowed. It was impossible to tell at what point, if any, he bent. *"De nada, señor."*

"Your master wishes me to drink with him tomorrow." Considerable gleaming of small eyes at this—but no conversation. "Where does the *Señor* Angel live?"

"Thees ees not far."

"How far?"

He shrugged. "Eet ees maybe two places, señor. Eet ees one place five, seex *kilómetros*. Eet ees wan odder place . . ." He counted on his great, brachydactylic stubs. ". . . four times upstair. The pant'ouse."

I told him to call for me at five tomorrow afternoon and eased him on his way. As I closed the door, I could not hear any footsteps. The hall floors were not carpeted. I looked out again, quietly, but he had gone. I feel better about two-hundred-pound men who can be heard walking on bare floors.

By the time I'd ordered my breakfast, the rain had stopped, but quick gusts of wind blew up at intervals out of the oppressive stillness. The waiter who brought the tray muttered about a *huracán* and put down a Spanish newspaper, from which I dug the idea that it was not expected to be much of a blow—as such things go in these parts. To a man on an unfriendly island, even moderately bad news is better than some of the stuff he dreams up.

My note from Carlos Angel didn't sweeten my feelings about meeting Fan-tan this afternoon, either. He'd probably followed me from my arrival at the airport. I ate my breakfast and went back to sleep.

Sometime later the wind woke me—whooping around the building and slapping disorderly chunks of rain against the windows. Around two o'clock, the rain eased off and the blow died down. A leaden, twilight quiet hung over the city. I wrote the hurricane off as a sudden squall—an error.

Fan-tan persisted in my mind and I wondered if I could get something more about him before we met again. I splashed over to the cafe and found Bert Lillio supervising the boarding up of the windows and the removal of the awnings. On the inside, the place was writhing with customers already. Bert came in and idled over to me. I asked him about my oriental pal.

"Fan-tan? He's not too bad a guy, Doc, as they run locally. He's a hustler, of course—but who isn't around here?"

"He got a job? Anything you could call a job?"

"I don't know—he does this and that. Fan-tan's been around five, six years, now, and always seems to do pretty good. I know he owns a taxicab some guy drives for him on commission. He's got some men selling lottery tickets. Probably got a woman staked out somewhere. You know how it is . . ."

"He's sure loaded with information."

"Why not? It doesn't cost him anything to keep his ears open." Bert laughed. "He sell you some?"

"A sample, yes. I've got him doing some—research for me. It's a sort of touchy thing, Bert. Nothing too serious, you understand—just a bit of local gossip that might be the difference between an ordinary book and—well, a rather sensational one."

"Be good if you hit the real big time, eh?"

"That's right—maybe pictures and stuff. You know."

"Sure." He shouted some directions at a couple of waiters who were hauling in a sign. "I don't think you need worry about Fan-tan, Doc. He has the trick of staying out of trouble—never gets in over his head. I told him you're an important guy in New York."

"That'll cost me."

"Maybe. But important guys get along right good in Havana."

I strolled back to the hotel and puzzled around my room for a while. At around four-thirty, I went down and had a drink at the bar. The maidenly monster was nowhere to be seen, though

I felt that I wouldn't be long out from under his flat eyes. The rain had quit again, but the storm-littered courtyard I could see from my stool reminded me that this would be the eye—the quiet center of the *huracán*. It would be as bad—or worse—again. I'd need to get someplace where I could spend a couple of pleasant hours before it hit. I had no desire to spend them in the hotel on top of which rested the Angel pant'ouse.

Since I was to meet Fan-tan at Lillio's place, I wandered over there. The joint was going full blast, loaded with happily storm-stranded visitors. Bert was squeaking his rubber heels around corners, so I sat at the bar until he saw me. He paused, mopped his forehead . . .

"Whyn't you go upstairs, Doc?"

"What's upstairs?"

"Nice, small bar. No band. No tourists. It's special."

So I landed upstairs. It was better than the headwaiter's brief plug. Good, comfortable chairs, quiet service, and only half a dozen people around. From someplace I heard the drone of orderly voices in the hush-click-murmur cadence that says roulette. I ordered some canapés and a drink.

It was pretty lonesome. Katie, according to her schedule, would be spending the week end with some people in Connecticut who make her paint fences and dig gardens in return for her beer and skittles. I had a yen to call Eddie and have him inform the local *jefe* that I am a nice guy and have only the pleasantest feelings about the Cuban people.

The wind started whining outside, rattling and banging the loosely hung shutters of the old building. But no rain came, yet. We were working our way back to the other edge of the storm. The room downstairs was full of noise and excited stirrings. I wondered if the mob which had arrived so quickly when the weather let up would leave as fast. My food came and I fooled around with it, killing time.

After a while the bartender walked over and said, "You Doc?"

"Yes. Why?"

"Mr. Lillio says there's a man downstairs to see you."

"He say who it was?"

"Fella you talked to last night. Lillio will send him up when you say—if you want to see him."

"Thanks. I'll see him now."

The barman went away. A party of cardplayers folded up and left the room. Two other tables were occupied—a man reading a newspaper and a couple intent on each other. Fan-tan came up the stairs and ambled across to me with his hat in his hand and still wearing the post-card leer.

"Looks like we might have some weather, Mr. Connor."

"Yeah. Doesn't it!" Fan-tan stood, grinning, in his pale blue tropical suit. "Will you sit down and have a double gin?"

"I'll sit down. You can give me a rain check on the double gin." He took his time disposing of his hat and getting himself seated. The bartender started across and I waved him back. Fan-tan produced a pair of horn-rimmed spectacles, put them on, and beamed at me. "I see your pal Pedro is waiting for you."

"Pedro?"

"The Angel family hatchet man."

"Oh." What a small world! "He'll get himself wet."

"Pedro? Outside? Never! He's in the kitchen eating American style."

"I see. Is he—close to the management or something?"

"Pedro isn't that complicated. He's close to food—and to you, of course. Nobody had to tell Pete to hang around the kitchen, but some of the Angels had to tell him to hang around you. What did you do to them? Carlos is the only one in town—"

"How much is it worth to you, Fan-tan?"

The guy laughed—a good hearty yok at himself. "It could be worth something, at that. Maybe I could peddle it."

"Is that what you came to see me about? To find out if I had anything you could peddle?" I felt, then, that I might have made a bad blunder in letting this guy get so close to the truth. Yet how could I have found any of Chapin's tracks without talking about the Bolado boy to someone?

The Chinese cocked his head to one side and fiddled with a paper of matches. I watched him and decided I'd had no choice.

If he'd been sent after me by the Angels—by Little Willie—or by Chapin, it didn't make much difference. It was the right direction and I had to follow it. He finally said, "Something to peddle, Doc? Mebbeso, as my unenlightened brethren say, mebbeso. With Pedro shagging you around, I figured you might be working for one of the Angel boys."

"I'm not." He hadn't said it coyly—just suggested it as a perfectly natural possibility. "Pedro is an added starter."

"He is a very bad lad." Fan-tan sat silent and tore matches out of the paper book. After a while he threw the holder down and brushed the matches into a pile. "Buzz Chapin is a very bad lad, too."

"I know."

Then the man did a strange thing—or what seemed strange for him, at least. He put two American twenty-dollar bills on the table in front of me. "I can't take your money, Doc."

I decided to take the surprises in the order of their importance at the moment. "Doc?"

"Doc." He smiled pleasantly. "I won't play games with you. There are several ways to explain why I can't help you. The one which would make the most sense to you—and save trouble all around—is that I have sold my services to a higher bidder."

"All right. Now how about the 'Doc'?"

"You're too modest. It wasn't your local fame that tipped me off, though. I am a very resourceful guy, Doc. I looked you up in the Manhattan telephone directory. Among the James Connors was Dr. James Cardigan Connor." He grinned. "From there on, I needed only to remember what I'd read in the local press within the last day or two. You see, the Anita Ferrier story was of special interest to us all in Havana."

"Hell! I hadn't thought of that."

"There are some other things you haven't thought of, too."

"And what are those?"

"First, a couple of the Angel boys are pretty rugged citizens. I don't say they run the town or anything like that. They don't. Havana is as well run as most cities where people come to play. But they have a lot of interests—and a lot of influence."

"So?" The man was getting too close to the mark and I didn't know whether to like it or not. It was what I came down for, of course—but it seemed reasonably important, also, to get back; He looked up quickly, as though surprised.

"So? So they get annoyed with people who have ideas about embarrassing them."

"Why would that concern me? I asked you about a guy named Chapin." I decided I might as well get it cleaned up then as any time.

He smiled. "Sure, Doc. You asked about a guy named Chapin—and a guy named Chapin asked me about a guy named Caesar. Caesar's boy was drowned in a fishing accident some years ago. No one has ever seriously connected the kid's death with a little freight boat which was tied up near where his body washed in. That included me—"

"You were around here then?"

He pushed the pile of paper matches around the table. "Off and on, Doc. I was nineteen." The wind had started to pour it on—heaving grape-sized blobs of rain at the windows. "It looks like now maybe Chapin has found out something—unpleasant."

"Like what?"

"Like whatever brought you down here in such a hurry after Anita Ferrier's death, pal. I took your money to find out more about that. I gave it back because either I don't want any part of you—or I've already been paid to—help you."

Oriental complexities sound strange in Brooklyn accent. "Somebody might have paid you to help *me?* I don't understand."

Fan-tan shrugged his heavy shoulders. "To help you or hinder you. That depends on what you want here."

I saw only one out. I could get into trouble with theories and suspicions. "I want to find out who killed Anita Ferrier."

He sat perfectly still long enough to sort out whatever pieces of our relationship he was considering. "So do I, Doc."

"That's what you were paid for?"

"No. I didn't know it, but I guess that's what I was paid to prevent."

The building rasped and creaked in the storm. You couldn't see out any more. It looked like somebody was playing a hose on the windows. Fan-tan said, "How you going to get back to the hotel?"

"Why don't we wait until it blows over?"

He laughed. "The building?" There was no more noise from downstairs. The people had probably gone long ago. The water was running down the edges of the window frames, soaking the carpet. "I've got a car inside about a block from here."

"Who paid you, Fan-tan?"

He had stood up. He turned and looked down. "Anita Ferrier, Doc. Let's go."

11

We started down the stairs. A rending crash somewhere in the rear of the place hurried us on our way. Fan-tan, over his shoulder, hollered, "The kitchen blew off last year."

The first floor was deserted except for a barman locking up the stock and an old fellow with a watchman's clock. The rain was driving against the outer doors and there was no one, beyond them, in the street. The lights in the café were mostly out—a couple of dirty working bulbs set up between the tables drove the room farther into shadow. What light there was outside was darkly forbidding. I took a deep breath and followed Fan-tan to the door. A gust swung us around and we ducked back into the doorway again.

Some people came by—three or four raincoated figures huddled together, heads down against the slapping wetness. We struggled to the corner behind them. At the corner another blast threw us against the building and the people disappeared into the driving mass ahead. Fan-tan took hold of my arm, yanked me aside. A sheet of corrugated steel hit the street and scraped along past us. "Half a block now, Doc."

Two sopping minutes later we were in a concrete garage building. While I was stamping the excess water off me, I heard my companion say, "Hi, Pete!"

The little square man was sitting in the corner—completely dry. He opened his eyes enough to indicate consciousness, removed his large hat, and nodded.

"Señor."

Then, very deliberately, he replaced his hat, turned his head in my direction, arose, removed his hat again, bowed deeply. Sat down again.

"Señor!"

Fan-tan laughed. "There you have our comparative social standings, Doc." He took my arm and we walked toward the back of the garage, called loudly for somebody back there. Then he spoke softly to me. "That *zopenco* will have a car here. I want to lose him."

"What difference would it make if you just take me to the hotel?"

"I've changed my mind about going to the hotel. I think we should make a call." There was no threat in his voice, but I wasn't ready to accept any invitations from the guy.

"Call? On whom?"

"On the only person in Havana, I suspect, who can give you a lead to the man that killed Anita Ferrier." A boy emerged from some hole in the rear, called to Fan-tan, and started to move cars. "Look, Doc, I'd better tell you some stuff quick. I've got a hunch we can't stall any more—"

"Why? Not that I want to stall, but what's the pressure?"

"The pressure is Carlos Angel—and that joker up front. I can lose him in this mess—and the person we want to see is sure to be indoors. I can lose Pete once. Then, tomorrow, Angel will have a dozen guys on us—up to and including the cops." A dark blue Ford pulled up. I looked for the maidenly monster, Pedro. He had disappeared. Fan-tan said something to the boy in Spanish and we got aboard hurriedly—the lad running on ahead to open the doors to let us crawl out into the weather. As we turned into the street, I did not hear the doors slide shut and took it for granted Pete would be next out.

Fan-tan splashed along the street for not more than fifty yards, then suddenly turned into an alley. We could see an entire block of its partially sheltered length and we took full advantage of it—roared through in second and whipped down the next street below. I looked back. The sheet of water had closed behind us. I said, "Neat!"

"Yeah. It had to be quick or I'd have been at it for an hour. I drove cab here a couple of years."

"You were going to tell me some things . . ."

He didn't say anything for a few moments. We hooked out into El Prado to get off the cobblestones. The trees along the way seemed to be coming to pieces and a branch draped over our hood briefly, then blew away. We turned off the boulevard and splashed through a back street which was a foot deep in water. Fan-tan said, "We'll get some shelter first—then talk."

I wasn't happy about it, but sat in sodden discomfort through several more streets. Then, suddenly, we pulled up in front of the double doors of another garage building and Fan-tan sounded the horn—a throaty, intermittent gargle which brought immediate action on the doors. We drove in. Fan-tan said something to a little dark man, who promptly climbed into a taxicab and started the motor. As we stepped out Fan-tan said, "All right, Doc, I'll make it quick. Pete will turn up here within the next few minutes sure. That's my cab and he knows where I keep it—or can find out.

"Here's the story. I told you I was around here when the Bolado thing happened. I was. I was engineer and crew for Jack Ferrier. I loved the guy—and I worshiped the woman he married. I didn't even know her very well, but I was a punk kid and she was the only good woman I'd ever been around much, except my family, Stateside. I'd seen the Bolado kid here and there, but never connected his death with the boat or anybody around her.

"When Chapin came here and started to ask questions about the boat, somebody sent him to me. Even then I didn't tie it up. Before he left, he asked me some questions about the Angel family. I stalled him off and wrote Anita Ferrier about him—"

"Oh?" It had been as simple as that! "Look, Fan-tan, did she write back and ask you to find out what Chapin had been after?"

"Yes. She even enclosed what she called 'expense money'—she was pretty much upset. You see, now?"

"Were you able to tell her what Chapin was after?"

He looked straight into my face—stared for an instant as if trying to decide whether to lie to me. I don't think he did. "No. For two reasons, Doc; one, because I couldn't find out exactly; the other, because she was dead—and you were here—before I could figure out *how* to find out."

"You think you know, now?"

"Yeah." He headed me toward the cab. "Let's go."

We piled in, Fan-tan gave the driver an address I couldn't hear, and we bucked out into the storm, headed directly at its teeth for several blocks. Quite a lot of it came in at the seams of the old cab. The driver and Fan-tan exchanged some loud colloquy, apparently on the subject of the road, because when the shouting had subsided Fan-tan said, "It's a couple of miles out. We may hit a wash or two."

We hit several—ploughed through in cascades of water and mud to the earnest cursing of the little driver. A scraggly farmhouse showed up out of the rain to our right and Fantan yelled to turn in—then yelled not to, as he recognized the sort of rut that ran to the place. The driver slowed, skidded, and stopped almost to his hubs in goo—sat and raised his arms to heaven in protest beyond his exhausted vocabulary. We stepped out and wallowed our way to the door.

A young girl welcomed us with wide, curious eyes. Fantan said something which included the words *mama grande* which, I find, is an Americanism. Grandma was at home—a lean, hawk-faced old woman who might have been any age between eighty and ninety. She sat in a great chair—the only solid piece of furniture in the room. An oil lamp burned on a table beside her, sharply outlined the crinkled vellum restraining the jutting cheek and jaw. Fan-tan came close to her.

"You know me, *nana?*" I wondered that he spoke in English.

She answered, almost without accent. "I do not see you well, *señor*. You are Chinese—that much I see." She made a small gesture with her thin hand. "I have known many Chinese."

"I am Charley Toy, *nana.*"

The old woman dropped her head and brooded over her folded hands. "Charley Toy." A small amusement touched the lines of her mouth. "Charley Toy!" Her laugh was dry, rough. "Perhaps the years have tamed you, too, Charley. If so, I am glad to see you. If not, I shall lock my granddaughter in her room and call the police. You are well?"

"I am well, indeed, thank you, *nana,* and I am glad to see you." The girl shyly placed chairs for us. Fan-tan performed an exaggeratedly respectful bow in thanks, gestured the woman's attention to it. "Also, as you see, I am now a *caballero.*"

"Very well. You exaggerate, but you do not, at least, offer to sing bawdy sailor songs such as you taught my Angels. Please be seated."

"Thank you, *nana.* I present the Doctor Connor."

She inclined her head. "You are *médico?*"

I said I was and Fan-tan did the build-up. "A celebrated *médico,* nana, who has come to us from New York on a sad errand."

"I have had sufficient sadness. I have, also, a fool for a *médico.* One who gives very small pills for very great pain. Perhaps the Doctor, your friend, gives pills of a sufficiently large size?"

Fan-tan bowed deeply. "There is no giver of larger pills in New York, *nana*—isn't that true, my friend?"

I did some bowing, too. "It is quite true—with one exception. For a great pain in the region of the left arm and of the chest beneath the arm, I give pills of small size and great strength."

The woman peered eagerly at me, her black eyes squinted. With her right hand she stroked her left arm absently. "Perhaps they are not all *tontos,* these *médicos.* I have such a pain."

"Have you heard recently from Anita, *nana?*" Fan-tan touched her hand.

"Anita? I hear from her only at *Pascua de Navidad*—why do you ask, Charley?"

The girl stood behind her grandmother's chair, held fingers to her lips in warning. "The Doctor is Anita's friend. That is why he wished to know you, as well. She and her brothers have told him many tales of the old days—and of their beloved *nana.*"

From outside, the cab motor roared across the wind as the driver ground his way back to the road. The lamp guttered and flared against a sharp draft from somewhere in the cottage. The old woman pulled her shawl more closely around her shoulders. She said, "There were many tales to tell."

"There has been *chisme* in New York, *nana*—unpleasant talk regarding one of the old tales. Anita is not happy with it." Fan-tan spoke quietly.

"So she has let me understand." A suspicious reserve came over the woman.

"But you said you hadn't heard from her since Christmas."

"I have letters from Anita at Christmas. Letters and *rega-los*—with money for my old age. At no other time do I hear from her—directly."

Fan-tan was urgent. "But indirectly, *nana*. Have you heard from her?"

A puzzled expression passed over her face—relieved by some sudden decision. "What do you wish to learn, Charley Toy?"

"There has been talk of Jack Ferrier's boat and of—an accident." Fan-tan took on the post-card leer—leaned toward her. "But then, you are probably too old to remember such things."

"You are right. I am too old. I have forgotten them." She was pleased to have been provided so simple a solution.

"So you do not remember who was on the boat that day, *nana?*"

"You, Charley—you were on the boat. And Ferrier. He, too."

"But not at the right time. You must have thought about it!"

"I have thought about it, yes." She waited, firm-lipped and erect.

Fan-tan eased off a little. I began to have more respect for his tactics. "How could such tales have been started, *nana?*"

"Easily enough. That dreadful *borracho,* Caesar—the boy's father—he has babbled, when he was drunk, that the accident was due to the carelessness of one of my boys." The woman glanced about the room as though afraid to be overheard. "It is not true, of course."

"Does he mention which of the boys it could have been?"

She was quick enough. "How could he? It was none of them."

"How do you know?" When she didn't answer, Fan-tan said, "One of the boys must have been aboard, *nana*. I have heard the gossip myself. One other person has heard it, too, and he has caused Anita great unhappiness."

The bony hands moved impatiently in her lap. "I do not wish to talk with you about it, Charley Toy. Nor with the good Doctor of the large pills. Whatever I have known of these matters, my Anita knows also. If she wishes you to know of them, she will tell you."

"Your Anita is dead, *nana*." It was not without sympathy.

The girl uttered a small cry, a breathless "No—no!" The old woman raised her head. Her eyes hardened to a fierce gleam. Her fingers clawed at her skirt. Then, quite peacefully, she said, "If she is dead, she will have no more concern for these things. She will be with God."

The right hand was raised to her breast. Slowly she moved it to her left arm and held it there. A steady dripping of water inside the house beat a measured rhythm against the harsh rushing of the wind.

Neither Fan-tan nor I said anything—sat quietly, held by the fearful intensity of the woman's mood. I had the feeling she was praying as she rocked forward and back, her head bent, her eyes at our feet. Perhaps she was dreaming of the days of her brood of dark Angels, instead, or wondering what trouble she had brought upon herself by some unguarded words before Buzz Chapin. Perhaps she was just being old and in pain.

Then she spoke, addressing her words to her bony knees. She spoke haltingly and in Spanish words so softly uttered that Fan-tan leaned forward to listen. He repeated the phrases in English as though enchanted by the sounds he heard.

"'They would turn upon him—and devour him—they would destroy him—he is as a beautiful child among them . . .'"

Fan-tan spoke sharply. "Who, *nana*, who? Who is as a child among them?"

The old woman raised her head, her dark eyes found his—peered blankly in the lamplight.

"Who, *nana?* Tell us!"

"Jesus Christ our Lord."

Fan-tan leaned back. "It's no use, Doc." Then, to the woman, "We need to know everything about the accident, *nana*. It is for Anita's good."

"Anita is dead, Charley Toy. You, yourself, have told me so. She is no longer in need of your help."

I said, "Anita had heard stories of signed papers, *madama*, and of statements given by someone here in Havana." Fantan glanced quickly at me and, as quickly, away. "Is there someone else here who might know so much of the—unfortunate affair?"

"Papers? Statements? What do I care for these things?" She fairly spat the words at me. *"Madre de Dios! Sí!—Sí!*—I have signed papers for the *abogado!* I have never before spoken of these things and I will never speak of them again. I have forgotten them!"

Fan-tan shouted right back. "The *abogado!* When did you do this?" Turned his head to me. *"Abogado.* That's a lawyer, Doc. The son-of-a-bitch posed as a lawyer!"

"Go away! Go away, Charley Toy!" She bowed her head until her angular chin rested on her breast. "Go away! I wish to weep."

Fan-tan turned to me. "There's Chapin's source, Doc. You see how impossible it would be for anyone else, now."

I said, "All right. I'm satisfied. Let's get back."

The girl came in with a little box and held it out to the old woman. Fan-tan spoke very gently, "Good-by, *nana.*" We re-treated to the door. We heard the girl say, *"Las pildoras, mama grande."*

The old woman took a small pill for her great pain.

12

MONDAY EVENING, OCTOBER 8

I am taking the morning plane back to New York.

I have learned a lot—and nothing. Today, with the help of an elderly attorney—a semiretired veteran of several administrations—I pieced together a considerable biography of the various Angels. The old gentleman, recommended, incidentally, by Fan-tan, amplified his vigorous memory with several hours of research among old newspaper files and court records. For fifty American dollars, I bought myself thirty pages of complete confusion, scrawled in a school notebook.

As might be expected of a wealthy, somewhat arrogant, and very lively family of boys, the record of the pubescent Angels contains evidences of minor crises ranging from alcoholic pranks to sternly suppressed tales of emotional involvement in high quarters. There was enough, in fact, to warrant the alert winging from New York of any given Angel in protest of somebody's shuffling about in his past.

How much—and which—of this has to do with Little Willie I can't, of course, determine at the moment. The records of the Bolado investigation—a rather casual procedure as it was recorded—ascribe Willie's probable savagery to the ripping, needle teeth of barracuda and the pounding of the surf. Because the boat had been lying suggestively near, Ferrier and Charley Toy, it seems, had been gently questioned and dismissed from mind. Because the boat's tender had been found well beached in its customary place, it was quite obvious that young Bolado

either had nothing to do with the boat whatever, or had fool-
ishly attempted to swim out to it. The possibility that someone
had rowed him out, killed him, and chucked him overboard
appears to have been overlooked or rejected—on the basis, in
all likelihood, that the boy's social status hardly warranted so
much planned activity on the part of his betters.

Ferrier's decision to let well enough alone for the protection
of his own prospective Angel had put an end to the investigation—leaving him forever exposed to serious charges if he felt
it necessary to disclose his actions. I neglected to inquire about
any Cuban version of the statute of limitations. It was not a
matter of reopening the Bolado affair to legal procedures. It was
a matter of learning a name—of gently prying from a stubborn,
dying old woman a hint as to which of her Angels took—and
furtively replaced—the keys that day, twenty years ago.

I had planned, of course, to go back to her when she'd finished her weeping over the death of her Anita, but had little
hope of convincing her that one of her beloved Angel men had
destroyed his sister. Apparently Fan-tan had planned to talk
with her again, too. He called me at four this afternoon to say
that *nana* had finished her weeping, at last.

She had died during the night.

I feel certain that, even in the face of Chapin's pose as Anita's attorney, she had kept the name to herself. If she had told
Anita—which she had suggested she had done—and Anita, in
turn, had revealed her knowledge to one of her brothers, it is
still a secret.

Little Willie won't be driven from hiding by frontal assault.
Unless Eddie Marsh and his rural associates come up with physical evidence against one of the Angel brothers, Willie will
crouch, fearful but unchallenged, in his dark, accustomed corner. He has, in all probability, committed two murders. He may
have been restrained from committing a dozen.

He must, in my opinion, be invited to commit another.

He will present himself, screaming and scratching, only in
the face of extreme—and possibly specific—pressures. Perhaps

there's a symbol like *ant hill* or *tortilla* or, by this time, *Bolado* which will loose his infantile fury. Whatever it is, I must learn it.

I wonder what would happen to Chapin if I suggested to each of the brothers Angel that Buzz knew who had been on the boat that day. To Chapin or, of course, to me . . .

It is a very unpleasant idea. I think that, before I play games with even such trifling lives as Chapin's and mine, I'll try everything else. Perhaps Eddie will have already apprehended the guilty party—the wayfaring stranger—and clapped him into the cooler. Then I'll have been on an all-expense vacation tour— won in Ferrier's unhappy quiz show in reverse where the prizes are awarded for asking, rather than answering, questions.

One thing is certain. None of the information which is in my possession constitutes what Marsh would classify as evidence. It is hearsay and inference. If Buzz Chapin has an alibi for the night of Anita's death, the implications of his blackmail cease to have any direct bearing on the murder. It was, in my opinion, strictly a family affair—precipitated, perhaps, by Chapin's action, but sprung from tensions long ago set up.

I've been trying to decide if I learned anything from my meeting, this afternoon, with the second eldest Angel brother. It's been raining again, today, and pretty dismal. Promptly at five a timid knock came at my door and the maidenly monster stood, hat in hand and beaming . . .

"The *señor* is ready?"

When I went for my hat and coat, he said, "We do not go outside, *señor.*"

"Oh? The penthouse?"

"Oyeh, *señor.* The pant'ouse." He bowed, then raised his eyes to the ceiling. "Four times upward."

I followed the man into the hall, curious about the noiseless walking I'd noted yesterday. Damned if he wasn't equipped with caterpillar treads. His short legs rolled him along from gently placed heel to lifting toe in a continuous glide. It would have looked funny—if it hadn't looked so menacing.

He crowded the lower four feet of the elevator, gave me the rest. At the top floor we emerged into a beautifully appointed hall. The man hesitated—rapped. Carlos Angel came to the door.

"Good afternoon, Doctor. It was kind of you to come. Enter, please?'

I got shed of the amenities as we walked through a second small hall and across a tremendous room which windowed a broad picture of the rain-drenched city and the piled-up harbor. The squat Pedro had disappeared behind us, undoubtedly through an alternate door. At a broad gesture from Carlos, I sat—deep and soft.

"I have bourbon, Doctor . . ."

"You seem to know my tastes, Mr. Angel."

"You are a horseman, are you not?" He smiled pleasantly. "In such a case, one would not guess otherwise."

I watched him fix the drinks—ascetically lean, dark, thinly mustached, and with an efficient grace in his movements. Jack Ferrier's story would make him about forty. When we'd settled on the proportions, he placed the highballs on a small table between us and sat across from me. I gave my glass a token hitch upward, nodded, and waited him out. It was his lead.

"First, Doctor, to discharge a small responsibility." Angel's dark eyes were grave. "I am instructed to inform you that the inquest into my sister's death will be held on Wednesday and that your presence will be necessary—perhaps I should say *advisable,* rather, since a deposition of certain facts will suffice if your business here is sufficiently pressing."

I felt that he had hit not less than two birds with his first stone, a shot which suggested careful rehearsal. "My business here is completed. That is, unless this meeting with you brings out some further need for my presence in Havana." Which was strictly ad lib—but in the spirit of getting on with it by indirection. Carlos acknowledged approval with a small gesture of his tall glass. "I feel quite certain that nothing I shall say would—extend your visit, Dr. Connor."

He managed to convey *get the hell out of town—or else* with consistent delicacy. It seemed time to haul the conversation down to a level where I could handle it more comfortably. "You will be required at the inquest, too, won't you?"

"Yes." He took a swallow of his drink while he decided where this led. "Yes. I had some little difficulty in getting permission to leave."

"I'm surprised they let you go."

"And I'm surprised they let you go, Doctor. You seem to have been a most important factor."

I wondered at my sudden importance. "Feeney didn't appear to think so, Mr. Angel. After I'd presented my testimony to him, he lost all interest in me. Perhaps there were—further developments?"

The thin, dark man put his glass carefully on the table. "The developments do not concern Feeney, Doctor."

Just like that. It was heavy with implication—a quiet, unmistakable approach to the business of the meeting. I said, "But you suggest they concern me?"

"That is quite right. They concern you." He opened a handsome silver humidor and gestured toward it—took out a cigar as I moved my hand in as gracious refusal as I could muster without breaking in. "Perhaps you will tell me why you came here?"

I had a lot of sudden and very insistent thoughts. They all needed rapid consideration and clamored for it. While that was going on, I said, "Perhaps I shall."

A door opened and the chunky Pedro tanked in with a tray of small sandwiches which he placed on another table. He earned the table to us, set it down, and rolled out of the room. Angel might not have seen him. "You see, Dr. Connor, there are some—aspects—of the relationship between us all that have, so far, escaped the attention of the police."

"And you feel that they should be called to Feeney's attention? Or Lieutenant Marsh's?" I thought I was baiting him a little.

He looked directly at me. "That—specifically—is what I propose to find out."

He was giving me time—and it wasn't doing me any good. I either had to tell him what I'd come to Havana for—or tell him it was none of his business. I decided the best thing to do was to tell him just that. "Mr. Angel; I'll not be childish enough to suggest that I am in Cuba to see the sights. I am here to investigate some factors which might have had to do with the death of your sister." He took a quick breath and leaned toward me. I said, "Wait, please. You have placed me in a position where I must either tell you things which I consider—shouldn't be discussed at this time—or tell you nothing." After that I couldn't hold him off . . .

"Why? Because, in some way, you believe me—suspect?"

"No. Because I can't accept the police's 'tramp out of the woods' hypothesis until some of those relationships of which you spoke have been cleared up."

He picked up his glass and examined it thoughtfully. "I see."

"Actually, Mr. Angel, it might be most helpful if you could see. You spoke in your note of the possibility of injuring innocent persons. I am very conscious of that possibility."

"Perhaps, then, you are equally conscious of the possibility that a brutal murderer might go unpunished in the process, Doctor."

"That seems to suggest that you don't accept the tramp theory, either."

"But I do, you see. I am—bitterly eager to accept the tramp theory. We all are, of course." He glanced sharply at me to see that I had the full implication of his remark. "It is not a pleasant thing to feel that such an act could have been performed by one of the—family."

"The servants . . ."

"Impossible, Doctor. They have cleared each other to the complete satisfaction of the police. It was not one of the servants."

"Have you any—fears—as to the possible killer?"

"Fears?" He frowned a moment. "Fears is the proper term." Carlos Angel stood up and walked, with his glass in hand, to the broad window—stared out at the steady rain. "I have many fears. Fears of unnecessary and possibly scandalous publicity.

Fears of hasty and unjust public accusation. Fears of well-intentioned but disastrous blundering . . ."

"On my part?"

He didn't turn from the window. "Yes. On your part." Then he walked slowly back to face me. "I feel that I must add the fact that we are not all in agreement as to whether your interest is well intentioned, Doctor."

"Oh?" I held on pretty well—for me. Felt my capillaries collapsing, but I didn't yell. "Doesn't that call for some explanation, Angel?"

"I, for one, thought it did." He was very calm. "At least I thought enough of the idea to find sudden and pressing business reasons to come to Havana."

"I think I know how to answer your question, now."

"About why you came? All right, what's the answer?"

"It's none of your business."

Angel seemed unaffected. He smiled a little, as a matter of fact. "We get forward, Doctor." He sat down again with the air of a man who has accomplished something.

"How do we get forward?"

"Oh . . ." The drink snapped to the glass table top with some emphasis. "We've waded through considerable polite conversation and finally reached the point where two other men might have started. You suggested that you were not a child to tell me you'd come for the scenery. Let me assure you that I am not a child to expect you to tell me, at once, why you did come." He leaned forward toward me. "I was quite prepared for your refusal, Doctor—and I'm equally well prepared to get the information in my own way."

And I was quite prepared to hear him holler for Pedro and a hot soldering iron, too, but decided he'd put it off for a while. I said, "You suggested in your note that you knew why I came. Why ask, then?"

"Because, for a man of your intelligence, you puzzle me by having joined in some obscure enterprise with Jack Ferrier— and having accepted a fee for your services. I'd been given to understand that your interest in—"

"*Fee!*" I guess I hollered a bit, because Angel smiled, very much pleased. While I was trying not to sputter, he documented his claim.

"Ferrier's office made your reservations and paid for your tickets. Let's not start being childish after all our resolutions." He snapped it off. "You must understand, Doctor, that Ferrier's pretended interest in minor estate economies has little to do with his real purposes. You must also understand that the death of his wife—our sister—places him in almost complete control of our—interests." He looked steadily out of the big window for a few moments. "Unless, of course . . ."

"Unless what?"

"Obviously, unless he is unable to benefit by her estate."

"You don't seriously think Ferrier had anything to do with your sister's death, do you?" So he was bitterly eager to accept the tramp theory!

"Frankly, I do not know what to think. Ferrier was making a bitter and determined stand against us—not only in the stupid business of the racing stables, but in the operation of our plantation and shipping interests. I know only that he desperately wanted control and that, now, he has it."

I decided to lay a few cards on the table—face down, for the time being. "Look, Angel; if, as you say, the servants are all cleared and, for hypothetical purposes, we discard the tramp theory, it leaves only the family. May I ask, without offense, if you know of any reason why one of your brothers might have become violently angry at his sister?"

His black eyes widened, narrowed, burned into me before he spoke. "I do not." The man composed himself determinedly. "You will remember that the unhappy possibility of my sister's accidental death would have occurred often to us—and to our attorneys. If we had not protected her because of our devotion to her, please credit us with the less honorable motive, at least."

"Yes. It's a strong point." I neglected to add that Little Willie would not be interested in riches. "It would have had to be some violent and uncontrollable outburst, of course. Was Ferrier—or, possibly, one of your brothers—given to that sort of thing?"

It was tossed out as lightly as I could do it, but I held my breath and watched. Carlos Angel closed one hand, slowly and firmly. With the other he put down his cigar. The muscular lump of his lean jaw tensed and relaxed. He opened

his hand and picked up his drink. "I do not think so."

What dark memory passed through the man I can't say—nor whether the shadow concerned himself or another—but in the period before he spoke, he had recalled a bad dream. Perhaps he was seeing the dying Anita, groping her way from the barn to the vaguely remembered security of her fireside.

How can you tell?

After some time, he spoke again. "Jack Ferrier implied that he was involved in some sort of business transaction with you—said things, more than a week before Anita's death, which suggested that you were to be entrusted with some 'very touchy'—as he described them—family documents. What they were, he refused to say. I think he was being intentionally mysterious. Did you have possession of any such papers, Dr. Connor?"

"I did not."

"Do you have now?"

"No." At least I could answer those questions without jobbery—even expound on them. "Truck Snowden told me one of you had asked him about my character or something . . ."

"What did my sister want of you, Connor?"

"Shall I guess?"

"If you don't know, yes."

"She wanted to find out if some 'very touchy' family documents had been entrusted to me." Lord knows she'd searched my place often enough without finding them! "She didn't get around to asking me directly."

Angel got up again and walked to the window. He turned and leaned against the sill. "Connor, I followed you to Havana because I thought you were carrying Ferrier's limited power of attorney to act in certain matters of great interest to the Angel family. Instead, I find that you are industriously digging up gossip. You seem to have searched out Ferrier's old helper,

Charley Toy, and visited the woman who was our housekeeper for many years. Did you know that she died last night?"

"Yes."

"It's too bad you burdened her with the grief of my sister's death."

"I'm sorry it happened that way." Then, as an afterthought, "You saw her later, I suppose."

"Yes. I saw her later. She was very ill."

"You learned, then, what we discussed with her?"

"Of course." He reached back and pressed a small pearl button clipped to the edge of a refectory table behind the couch. I heard the buzzer somewhere in the back of the apartment. "I think we've accomplished our business, Doctor. When I wrote you the note, I felt that your errand here was of some importance to me. I see that it is not." He rose.

I stood up with him, a little puzzled by his casual dismissal of the Bolado affair. His smile was hard as he put his hands to his sides and bowed slightly.

He said, "If it were not so tragic, I'd find Ferrier's plight rather amusing . . ."

I didn't get it—at first. *"Ferrier's* plight?"

"Yes." Angel turned a little as the squat servant stood in the doorway. "He reckoned without your quaint sense of ethics, Doctor. He apparently has employed a man to prove he's a murderer!"

13

Actually, for the record, it's Tuesday morning—crowding three o'clock. The rain has stopped and the tail of the hurricane has blown itself out in sweeping the last clouds from the night sky. Outside my window—and through the very stones of the building—the thousand rumba drums are flailing at the last, scattered straws of a poor harvest, ruined by the storm. There is no triumph in the occasional crashing of the cash registers, and the lusty tenor in the hotel below sings only because it is not yet four o'clock.

The delayed excursion boats and the piled-up airline flights have departed and, in a few hours, I am contracted to spend some more of Jack Ferrier's money to follow them north. I have packed my belongings—including the thirty pages of answers to a lot of, thus far, unasked questions.

I am discouraged, reeking with self-pity—and nursing a considerable contusion on the side of my head. These, with a general malaise, won't let me get back to sleep, so I've unlimbered the portable again.

I got a couple of hours' sleep earlier, but—was interrupted. From the time I left Carlos Angel's place—snorting and fuming against the unreasonably logical quality of his viewpoint—I was followed. There was no doubt in my mind that the man was a professional, although he made no effort whatever to disguise his business from me. A small, neat man in a conservative gray suit who used his skill only to escape me when, as I did several times, I tried to talk to him.

I ate dinner in almost lone state at El Carib, hoping he'd show himself so I could ask Bert Lillio who he was. No go. He disappeared and reappeared exactly on schedule. He tagged me to the hotel, where I found Fan-tan waiting for me in the lobby. I took my Havana-wise Chinese friend for a walk—so the guy went completely professional on us and neither of us could even spot him. As we went back to the hotel, however, Fan-tan had an observation to make.

"Doc, I think your tail has outsmarted himself."

"Oh?"

"There's only one guy in Havana who's that cute—and your description fits. He's a cop."

"Why would I pick up a cop?"

Fan-tan laughed. We sat down again in the lobby. "It isn't too tough to do around here, for one reason or another. But you got yourself a very special cop. I don't think there's any question but you caught yourself the police department's gold-plated —and only—criminologist. They usually keep him in a glass case."

"But, for me, he's doing a routine surveillance job?"

"For you?" He glanced casually but carefully over the lobby. "You miss the point, my friend. For the Angels, Doc. To paraphrase, this guy speaks only to the *jefe* and the *jefe* speaks only to the Angels—or something. His name is Kelly."

"Kelly! He looks Spanish enough . . ."

"Why not? He's as Spanish as Paddy's *puerco*. The original Kelly probably started a revolution someplace—or finished one."

"Why would Carlos Angel have me followed?"

"I can make two guesses, Doc." Fan-tan grinned happily. "He either doesn't want anything to happen to you, or he does want something to happen to you. What's more, maybe it isn't Carlos. There's still a mess of Angels in New York."

"Cheerful prospect! I'm planning to go home tomorrow, so not too much can happen." I said it, I suppose, without conviction.

"Don't bask in that, pal. When stuff starts to happen around here, it goes for quick. The thing that bothers me is how I'm going to get you away from Kelly for an hour or so tonight."

"What for?"

Fan-tan scratched his head and put his hat on again. "Doc, I talked to old Caesar—the Bolado boy's father—and I think he's got something you want. He's a hell of a wino and couldn't be trusted with a quarter. But I still think he's got something. I want you to see him."

I puzzled for a moment, wondering what the lad's father could have been holding for more than twenty years—and why he would have kept it secret. "Sure I'll see him. Did he give you an idea of what he knows?"

"Absolutely not. He listened. I told him you wanted to know about the accident and that there was some money in it for him. The old man's not very bright."

I said, "All right. How can we work it?"

Fan-tan leaned toward me, spoke earnestly. "Look, Doc, Kelly won't follow me when I leave here, and even if he takes a notion to follow me, I can lose him. I don't believe he'll stick here after he thinks you're in for the night, either. He's too big for that. Suppose I send somebody after you about, say, midnight. I know the late-trick elevator boy. He'll take you down to the lower side door that comes out on the alley. I'll meet you there. Right?"

I didn't like it and said so. "It sounds too damned complicated."

"Leave it to me. I'll send the boy for you when it's clear—sometime around twelve."

I saw Fan-tan off and grumbled my way back to the room, where I occupied myself in recording what you have already read about my interview with Carlos Angel. I lay down around ten, fully clothed, and slept until somebody knocked on my door at twelve-twenty. I took a look at the clearing night, picked up my hat, and went to the door.

The elevator man said nothing at all—simply paraded down the hall to his car and waited for me to get in. We rode in silence to the lower level and he let me out, closing the door hurriedly and returning immediately to the lobby level. I looked around in the semi-darkened corridor. A shadow flowed out of the blackness of a side entry.

"O.K., Doc, let's go." Fan-tan moved into the light. "My cab's outside."

We hustled into the car and the driver took off with much peering around for following vehicles. After several miles of circuitous rambling, Fan-tan quit back-seating and gave an address. The guy at the wheel squawked something in Spanish, raised both hands to document a Latin shrug of resignation, then went back to driving. I asked Fan-tan what was eating the man.

"Our destination is just under seven blocks from the hotel." He was studying every corner, every' chance pedestrian, as we went along. "You realize, Doc, that this is the one place in Havana we mustn't be seen."

"Tying us up with the Bolado thing."

"That's right."

"But Carlos Angel knows why we saw the old woman yesterday."

Fan-tan spoke to the driver, who slowed down. "If Carlos sent the cop, Kelly, after us, it's probably O.K., Doc. If one of the others did, it isn't so good."

"How do you figure that?"

"Carlos has had a lot of time to get Kelly—or a dozen other guys—on you since you've been in town. His hatchet man, old Sneaky Pete, has been tagging after you from the first hour." He poked the driver and we pulled up at a dark corner. "I figure Carlos doesn't think the Bolado thing can do the family any damage."

"One of them knows, though . . ."

"That's what I mean. Let's go on foot from here." He gave a long list of rapid-fire instructions to the driver and collected a bottle from the front seat. We walked to the next corner and turned into a still darker and dirtier alley. Halfway through, Fan-tan looked carefully in both directions and led me hurriedly down a broken cement stair. A vague light showed at the edges

of the doorway. The Chinese rapped softly. Another door, somewhere within, creaked open and shuffling steps came toward us
from the hallway. They stopped—waited. Fan-tan spoke softly . . .

"Caesar?"

The door opened and a bulky, dark figure preceded us down
the hall to a lighted room beyond. Nothing was said. When we
came into the light of the room, I had my first look at Bolado's
father.

He had dressed himself in the remnants of a blue suit and
wore a white shirt, a black string tie, and no shoes. His dark
face was clean and shaven. He walked unsteadily and, as he
indicated the room's only two chairs, he restrained a convulsive
shudder.

He had made the big try—the wino was dreadfully and pain-
fully sober. Fan-tan put his bottle on the table. Caesar looked
at it and started to tremble.

I said, "You'd better give the guy a drink. He's about to fall
apart on you."

Fan-tan said something in Spanish and Caesar got two cups
and a glass from a cupboard. He held the cups in one hand and
they clattered a tragic habanera as he hurried them across the
room. I poured him a couple of ounces of whisky. He looked
at it in a vaguely puzzled way, tottered across to the cupboard,
and came back with a wine bottle. I thought he was going to
refuse the whisky, but he diluted it instead, with wine, carefully
filling the cup only halfway. Then he mastered it with both his
heavy, jerking hands and drank it.

So he had had something to drink in the room all the time,
but let it alone for probably four or five hours in anticipation
of our meeting! I have a couple of patients at the Clinic who
should have so important an engagement!

Caesar and Fan-tan exchanged some Spanish and the wino
took both bottles, set them on the floor, brought his cup, and
sat down, flat on the deck, with his drinking tools carefully
arrayed around him.

Fan-tan laughed. "I take it for granted you won't join the
party, Doc."

"I can drink it or leave it alone on occasion." I put my hat on the table and sat down. "Does this man speak any English?"

Caesar, himself, answered at least part of the question by looking up quickly and with suspicion while he listened for Fan-tan's reply. "With distinct limitations of vocabulary—"

The man on the floor said, "Talk Espanis'."

It took several minutes of rapid chattering to dispose of the question of which tongue would be the official language of the meeting. Fan-tan finally announced that he would take part only as interpreter and that I was to conduct the investigation. He added, "There's one point, Doc. This guy wouldn't open his mouth until I told him Anita Ferrier was dead."

"So? Then he wanted to talk?"

"Well, he didn't exactly want to talk, but, when I told him you were representing her—"

"Wait a minute! Suppose that statement should get to anybody in authority. That's not too good."

"Take it easy, Doc. You're representing her interests, aren't you?" Fan-tan crossed to where Caesar was sitting. "What do you want me to ask him?"

The man said, "Talk Espanis'."

"Ask him if he wishes to tell me something about his son's death—something he may not have told the police."

The reference to police in English appeared to frighten the old fellow. It required more Spanish colloquy from which I could recognize *accidente* and *por casualidad*. As the dialogue slowed to an occasional burst, Caesar concocted himself another drink. His manner became more sullen and the word *dinero* recurred in his grumblings. Fantan seemed in no hurry to translate and waited patiently.

I said, "He seems to have gotten around to money."

The man looked up from his drink—squinted at me. "Money. Oyes, money. You give me money like before."

"What's he mean, *like before?*"

Fan-tan turned a startled face to me. "This is it, Doc. Wait a minute!" He rolled off a very fast hunk of Spanish which featured *dinero*. There was some impassioned arm waving before I got the verdict.

"Doc, this guy has been paid twenty dollars American every month for more than twenty years!"

"Good Lord! By whom?"

"He says he doesn't know. I think he's telling the truth. He says that, after Bolado's body had been found, he went to the back door of the Angel home and talked to the woman—the *nana*—and she gave him some money. Since then he's received a twenty-dollar bill by mail every month."

"What did he tell *nana?*"

"That his son had been on the way to the Ferrier boat with an order of groceries the day he disappeared. He has an inbred fear of the police and went to the Angels' simply to ask about it—since, of course, it was an accident. Wait a minute . . ."

He addressed some more sharp questions at the man. The answers sounded sly or evasive—delivered with sort of a sheepish grin. Fan-tan said, "That makes sense, Doc. When this joker discovered he knew something that was worth money—he swears he didn't ask for it—but when the old lady gave him the dough, he decided to nurse the deal along. He went back the following month—and promptly got paid. That's how it started."

"But *nana* knew more than Caesar did about it, Fan-tan. I feel certain of that. The old lady knew who was with the boy that day—and so did Anita Ferrier."

"Caesar thinks Anita was sending the money . . ."

"Ask him if he got the twenty this month."

The answer was no, which was the reason, naturally enough, why he was willing to look for a new source of revenue as soon as he heard of Anita's death. I gave him twenty dollars. Further talk disclosed nothing more than the fact that the boy had headed for the boat, that day, expecting to earn half a dollar for taking a box of provisions out in the tender. It seems that Caesar had waited impatiently for the boy and his half dollar for two drunken days.

The rest of tonight's adventures were sudden, violent, and, for a time at least, pretty frightening. We had just come out into the dim alley from Caesar's place and were headed toward where we'd left the cab. Fan-tan was walking next to the buildings and I was groping my way along the uneven walk farther toward the gutter when I heard a fast step, a smothered exclamation, and a heavy, thudding blow. I turned and saw Fan-tan falling—borne down by a burly figure. A bare arm was under Fan-tan's chin and a knee was braced against his arched back. As I stepped in to help, somebody slugged me alongside the head and grabbed me around the neck. I felt the knee hit my spine and slammed my heel backward as hard as I could. It hit bone and I took advantage of it—broke away, stepped aside, and hooked deep and hard into the man's belly with my right hand. He doubled over and I swung an automatic left up and in. He went down.

Fan-tan and his man were on the walk in a vicious tangle of arms and legs, so I dove into the pile with some idea of breaking it up. All I accomplished was to invite my own attacker to jump on top of the three of us and mess things up worse than ever. However, the move must have got Fantan's windpipe free, because he let out a bellow that could be heard a mile off. I think I heard running footsteps before one of the guys sapped me.

I asked Fan-tan if he was all right. A man's voice said, "Fan-tan? Who the hell is Fan-tan?" Somebody put a light into my face. I tried to sit up and the man helped me. I said, "Fan-tan's a friend of mine. Who are you?"

"I am Captain Kelly—of the police."

"I thought you would have gone back to your glass case by this time."

"We don't like American visitors drunk in the streets—especially this street. What's this about a glass case?" He had a slight, pleasant accent.

"I am told that you are kept in a glass case at police headquarters and only taken out on most important occasions."

He laughed and helped me to my feet. Slapped at my hip pocket.

"Besides, I'm not drunk. I was mugged."

"But you still have your wallet, señor. I think you must be mistaken. A little disagreement with your friend—Fan-tan, perhaps?"

We walked along a few steps and I began to collect my wits. "You left me too soon tonight, Captain."

He didn't disagree. "Apparently, Doctor. When I thought you safely asleep, I returned to my—glass case."

We came to the corner where the cab had been. It was gone and, in its place, stood another car—obviously a police vehicle, complete with uniformed driver. Kelly loaded me in and sat beside me. "We'll go to the Serrano. Maybe this time you'll stay in bed."

I said, "Where's my friend?"

Kelly chuckled. "Fan-tan? He is a very cautious fellow, Doctor. He will be a long way off, by now, in his little taxi. I did not bother with him. He can take care of himself."

We pulled out of the narrow street and were on our way. "You know him, then, Captain?"

"*Claro!* Who in Havana doesn't? He is a wicked one, Charley Toy, but he does not break the law. For that reason he does not interest me."

"But, for some reason, I interest you. Why is that?"

"Ah! You interest a number of people here, Dr. Connor. The men who accosted you in the street seemed—violently interested in you."

"Why would they want to attack me?"

His shrug was audible. "To rob you, no doubt. They ran off—as did your Chinese friend—when I arrived. Is it possible that someone in Havana doesn't like you, Doctor?"

"It is very possible."

"Perhaps they were employed simply to frighten you. You need have no further worry, since you are leaving in the morning." He held a cigarette case toward me. I took one. An American brand. The car rolled up to the main door of the Serrano— all gay lights, rumba music, and nobody around. Kelly lighted our cigarettes and said, "One moment, Doctor. Is it your opinion—now that you have visited old Caesar—that Anita Angel Ferrier was murdered because of some—family difficulty?"

I weighed the possibilities and gambled on Kelly being as good a cop as he was supposed to be. If he was that sort, his question wouldn't be premised on pressure from anybody. I said, "Yes." Then, "Perhaps you'll tell me why you—well—why you could have had any reason to ask."

"It is rather simple. I am interested in my work as a career officer of police. For many years and through many changes of administration here in Cuba, the police have been rather too casual in their investigations. I feel that I am a representative of the new order. In my—glass case—I find opportunity to review instances in which we have dismissed matters without sufficient study. One such case—one which has stayed in my mind—was that of the boy, Bolado."

"How would that be connected with Anita Angel's death, Captain?"

The glare of the entrance lighted his little smile. "Little things, Doctor—a word here and there—persistent small gossip over the years. It comes a little closer than that, though, to me. You see, the dear old lady who has so long treasured some of the facts—and who carried them with her to her God last night—was my grandaunt. The young girl who lives with her is my cousin." He made a little gesture with his cigarette. "There never was enough to interest the police, anyway. Now there is nothing."

"So you had been informed that I was coming to Havana with the Bolado affair in mind?"

"No."

"Why were you following me, then?"

He laughed aloud. "I was very specially requested to see that you came to no bad end. I shall be most embarrassed when it becomes known that you were attacked."

"Jack Ferrier?"

"No. Not Ferrier at all. An old New York friend whom I have learned to know and respect through professional correspondence—Lieutenant Edward Marsh of the police."

14

The nearest rumba band is two blocks up Broadway and the nearest streetful of Spanish is some sixty blocks north. There is a cool hint of autumn in the air and the Yanks have won the Series. The mail has accumulated unimportantly and Katie has scolded—with occasional tender pattings of the bump on my head.

Eddie Marsh has also scolded, but was somewhat less gentle in his concern for my skull. He was curious, though, and I was able to bully him a little despite my weakened condition. The three of us had dinner together, as we often do when there's less going on—seldom when Eddie and I have a deal on foot. Katie has a tendency to rob our plotting of a certain amount of dignity by treating my part of it, at least, as some sort of adolescent play.

While we worked on a brace of very handsome mutton chops and baked potatoes, for each, I went over the whole business. Eddie had made it very clear, during the cocktails, that there was absolutely no physical evidence yet in the hands of the police which seemed to concern any individual yet known to them. From that point, I knew that I had no right to withhold anything from Marsh—even Jack Ferrier's interest in the matter. I told all.

The big cop resorted, when I'd finished, to his favorite analogy. "You've got a fine fence and no posts, Doc. If one of the Angel brothers killed his sister in a fit of temper—because she had something on him or for any other reason—he didn't leave any evidence against himself. When I talked with Captain Kelly over the phone, he said he thought you were trying to dig up something on the—what was it again?"

"Bolado."

"The Bolado accident . . ."

I wouldn't let him pass it over that easily. "Maybe it was an accident, Eddie. Maybe not."

"That's just another panel of your no-post fence. Officially, it is an accident. The record says so."

"Almost five thousand dollars in hush money in twenty years says it's not."

"If Anita Ferrier paid it—on the old woman's say-so—what does that leave you? They're both dead." Eddie glanced at Katie as though he were surprised she hadn't interrupted—which she promptly did.

"Why do you suppose they had somebody hit Doc over the head?"

Eddie snorted. "In the first place, there's absolutely no reason to believe that 'they' or anybody else 'had' somebody hit Doc over the head! The good doctor has, for years, to my knowledge, offered his so-called head in areas of human

society where such conkings are routine. He also makes a practice of fastening on some sort of weird preconception of a criminal situation and making everything fit it." He grinned happily at Katie. "I'm somewhat disappointed to find you supporting him in it, though."

I was a little miffed—although I'd listened to the same dull business for several years. "So you want to fold the thing up? Call it off?"

Katie said, "Now you're trying to bully him."

Marsh was pleased. "Isn't he just, though! I must remember not to let it spoil my chops."

"I wasn't bullying anybody. It's a fair question. I think one of the Angels is a psychopath. I think he has nursed a fear—and maybe a hatred—of his sister for twenty years. I don't think she intended to expose anything she might have known about him.

She wouldn't have protected him all these years and suddenly turned on him. I think—"

Katie said, "Question! Question! Will Eddie fold up?"

"We're not ready for the question, madam." Marsh growled it out through a mouthful of potato skins, which he relishes extravagantly. "The little man is still in debate. Go ahead, Doctor. What else do you think?"

"I think that this Angel brother—Little Willie—killed Anita Ferrier for the same reason he killed the Bolado boy. Frustration—humiliation—hell! It could be any one of a dozen childhood fixations and distortions—"

"Doc, darling . . ."

"All right, what?"

"It sounds too much like you to—to sound enough like it was very practical. Aren't all these Angel men pretty normal—I mean in business and all that?"

Eddie said, "Definitely. They may be a little screwy in their—what—well, social habits—but they've got too much dough to be just plain normal."

"Look! I'm not talking about how they *appear!* Their social habits, as you call them, Eddie, don't mean a thing. There was a guy out home named Timbrick, a few years ago, who got himself into the penitentiary for manslaughter—a fight. He was a steady, honest logger—saved his money and all that. Worked up to be foreman and was well respected."

"But he killed a guy."

"That's right. Apparently damned near got off. There'd been a good deal of provocation and what not. Anyway, a woman who did a lot of prison work got him paroled to her and she and Timbrick agreed he needed more education. The woman set about teaching him algebra. He was a conscientious student and tried hard. One night he couldn't work out a problem and it embarrassed him so much that he went down to her cellar, got the ax, and beat her brains out."

Katie never batted an eye. "Your small talk is something less than delicate. Are you suggesting that Anita was giving her brother algebra lessons in the barn?"

"Don't be hard on him, Katie." Eddie's voice was warm with human understanding. "I see his point. They've got no use for an ax around a horse barn, so the guy had to use what he could find."

I responded coldly—I hope. "I still think some more stuff, and you're going to hear it, or somebody else picks up the tab for all this fine food—"

"We'll listen." Duet.

"Both Charley Toy and Kelly told me there had been occasional gossip around Havana about the Ferrier boat and the Bolado kid. It referred more to Ferrier than to the Angels, I think, although the Angel boys were known to hang around the boat. Buzz Chapin heard the talk and set out to make somebody pay for it. He tackled Ferrier and got his cash. Ferrier tried to trap one of his brothers into coming to me—he didn't know which one, of course—and his wife got caught in the trap. She searched my place—still trying to protect whomever she'd been protecting for twenty years."

Marsh jumped in. "So the guy she'd been shielding kills her. It won't make sense, Doc."

Katie put her napkin on the table and reached for her bag. "Look, gentlemen, the woman who searched Doc's apartment—and who kept watch out in the street somewhere for hours on end—must have been pretty determined to do *something* to *somebody!* Maybe protect him—maybe hang him—I wouldn't know. It would be my guess that Anita Ferrier was convinced that her husband was aboard his boat that day."

I fairly hollered. "No! It can't be, Katie! Anita Ferrier was protecting her husband, all right, but she knew which of her brothers had killed the boy—and probably why. I think she was violently surprised to find that her husband was being black-mailed—which he actually was, of course, despite the fact that he'd written the note himself. She must have thought that one of the other brothers, not knowing the truth, had taken a notion to threaten Jack Ferrier."

Eddie said, "You mean a brother who'd had nothing to do with the Bolado affair?"

"That's right. Apparently Ferrier—or any of the Angels, for that matter—could have been aboard that day. The gossip which has come up from time to time in Havana might have suggested a shot in the dark at Ferrier."

Katie said, "But we know that nobody accused Ferrier—he'd written the note trying to smoke out the real—the person who was with the boy on the boat."

"Quite right. Anita wouldn't know that, though." I felt I was getting my own thinking straightened out, whether they agreed or not. "She would have gone directly to the brother she did know had been with Bolado and told him what was happening."

"One question, Doc." Eddie was waking up. "Do you think that the guy you call Little Willie knew she'd been protecting him?"

That would be it, of course. I'd hoped one of them would ask, because I figured it as the key to the whole business and wanted someone to mention it beside me. "I do not. I think she talked to him in the barn that night and, probably in her determination to bring it all out in a family conference, told Little Willie that she'd been paying off for him for twenty years. Little Willie must have been annoyed—and showed it."

Katie excused herself and went out to take care of her face. Eddie seemed quite serious for the first time. "Doc, that's a towering structure of supposition, but it just could be. Obviously we've got to do something about the Ferrier-Chapin thing—with Ferrier's co-operation, of course, and when it won't spill any possible developments on the killing." He pulled out his old black notebook. "This hypothesis of yours fits all the facts—such as they are. It at least makes the rather casual inter-family alibis for the time subject to more checking—"

"I don't think you'll get anyplace with physical facts. Maybe after you know who you want, yes. Not before."

"So what do we do about it?" Marsh is asking me!

"You—officially—go right on weighing and measuring. You keep the guy worried for fear he's forgotten something. In the meantime, I'm going to get Jack Ferrier's help in working over those five guys one at a time. If I get the right password—*cherry pie,* or some girl's name, or some incident one of them will re-member from long ago—the right one will blow up in my face."

"You and Freud! Isn't he a touch—discredited or something? Freud?"

"Let's say he's subject to—reinterpretation in some areas. He'll do for this one, if my guess is any good."

Eddie applauded the chef with a bread crust in the browned drippings. "If your guess is any good, pal, you'd better be damned sure there isn't a blunt object lying around."

15

Tonight I have set the whole thing up with Jack Ferrier. He says that the interpretation I gave Eddie Marsh has to be the right answer. Rather than being upset when I told him I'd confided in the Lieutenant, he seemed relieved.

"Marsh looks right to me, Doc. He's kept the thing as orderly and impersonal as anybody could have—what with my brothers-in-law shouting around and threatening to have every cop on the detail thrown off the force. The Lieutenant has kept his dignity—and his patience." Ferrier stared dismally at his highball. "If we get into something as vague and complex as it looks to be from here, I'd want Marsh around."

"So would I, Jack. He's factual as hell, but he's got imagination on his own time." I sorted out my thirty pages of stuff from the Havana *abogado*. "You want to go over this with me?"

"There might be something . . ."

More than an hour later we freshened the drinks and sat back to see where we'd arrived. I said, "Maybe you'd like to kind of ramble along about these men. You realize, of course, that the man you're looking for needn't show any great degree of instability in his day-to-day life . . ."

"I see that." He fooled with a cigarette and got himself settled. "One thing should be cleared up first. I don't know if Anita had been sending the money to Bolado's father. I'd have no way of knowing. She took care of her own checking account—

which was a fairly substantial one—and twenty dollars a month out of cash—you say it was always a bill?"

"So Caesar said—or, actually, so Fan-tan said he said."

"Fan-tan!" Ferrier smiled a bit wearily. "Charley Toy is a screwball of the first water, but he's fanatically honest with honest people. I wonder where he picked up that name?"

"That's what everybody around Havana calls him, now. Are you implying that Toy would be dishonest with dishonest people—maybe Chapin, possibly?"

"Definitely not. There might be some obscure way in which Charley hoped to bleed Chapin by informing Anita—but I doubt it. That would involve too much mental effort of him. I think you can accept what he had to say at face value."

"I did, as a matter of fact. How about the money to the old *nana?* Did you know your wife was sending that?"

"Yes. It was a perfectly natural thing to do—although, to my knowledge, she never asked her brothers to share in it. It could have been some form of loyalty insurance, but I'm certain she'd have taken care of the old lady anyway."

I was anxious to get on to some picture of the Angels. "What do you think of Carlos' attitude toward me in Havana?"

He thought a moment. "I'd say it was characteristic, Doc. He was afraid I'd sent you down to cover some estate matters for me. As you know, my wife's death brings up some rather complicated financial matters down there. If I'd known Carlos was going to fly to Cuba, I'd have had a reception committee of attorneys to meet him. The estate will not only be something of a mess, but, no matter how it works out, the end result will be damned unpopular with my brothers-in-law."

"Yet here I'm maintaining that one of them brought it on himself, Jack."

"If you're right—and I believe you must be—it only eliminates premeditation. Your theory requires an obscure, overpowering motive—suddenly aroused and suddenly spent." Ferrier stood up and stretched his legs, took a turn around the rug. He looked thoughtful enough for me to wait him out. "If we have to confide in anybody in the family, I suggest it be Carlos."

"Why?"

"Because he's mean. Because he's avaricious and greedy to the point where nothing in God's world would tempt him to jeopardize any substantial part of his material wealth." He whirled around and gestured passionately with his finger. "I'll guarantee that, if he thinks one of his brothers killed Anita, he'll find out who did it and hound him to the chair if it's the last thing he ever does. You know why, Doc?"

"Surely not any tenderness for his sister—if he's that sort."

"That's right. He'd do it because he'd get a quarter instead of a fifth of the brothers' share of the undivided part of the estate! He's a first-class heel—but he didn't kill Anita."

"Do you suggest we talk with him?"

"I have no idea what we should do—yet." With this, Ferrier's anger collapsed a little and he came back to his chair. "At the moment, I'm for a family conference—with the pressure on and the doors locked. Maybe get them all down to Cielito and lay it out for them."

"So—what would happen?" I didn't like the sound of it,

"How do I know what would happen? Something would happen—that's sure!" He shook his head. "Ramon, the eldest, would be fat and greasy about it. Unctuous, I think they call it. He's all right—not a bad guy at all, in fact—but he's a compromiser. He's even tried to fix up things more comfortably for me with his brothers.

"The noise, Doc, would come from the kid—Mariano. I say kid—he's thirty-seven, I think, but he's got a sort of starry-eyed thing about him. He was closest of any of the boys to Anita—loved her dearly and has been frantic about her death."

"What's he do?"

"Beside being a sort of partner in the sugar companies—with which he has nothing to do whatever—he is one of the world's few really good translators of Sanskrit."

"Good Lord! Sanskrit!"

"That's right. He's had three books of translations published and spends most of his time corresponding with students here and there."

My ears began to stand up some. Ferrier was describing a guy who had not only fled his language but actually had fled his century! "How would you like him for young Bolado's playmate, Jack?"

"No. In the first place, Bolado would have spanked him and sent him home. The boy—even then at like fifteen—was scrawny and unadventurous. He was the one who had to ask about everything on the boat three times before he could get up enough nerve to try it." Ferrier cocked his head to one side and looked at me. "Unless you've got some sort of psychiatric devices to make a fiend out of a shy friendly, undersized kid, I'd give up on Mariano."

"But he'd make the noise, you say. How? Would he be persistent about trying to find who killed his sister?"

"I think so. He has been, so far . . ."

"How about the others?"

"Juan and Alonso? They're the middling ones. I think Johnny's forty-one and Lonny's a couple of years younger. They are strongly contrasting—and conflicting—personalities. Johnny's a natural leader. He's quick and outspoken. You may remember that it was Juan who first brought out the fact that we'd been quarreling among ourselves—"

"I was impressed with him. Is he in the business?"

"In and out; Doc. He's one of the real horsemen among them—loves it—but, strangely enough, he's been one who'd side with me when the going got too rough. He'd like to cut the stable down to where the boys could handle it—if he didn't think it would collapse entirely. Johnny's pretty much all right, Doc."

"But you'd recommend Carlos as a confidant instead of Juan?"

"Yes—largely, however, for the reasons I gave you. I know Carlos wouldn't let his temper cost him anything."

"Juan's might?"

Ferrier considered that carefully. Finally he nodded. "Yes. Juan's might. He's got a quick, reckless temper. He damned near killed a—" He stopped suddenly. "I'd forgotten that."

"What?"

"Johnny almost got in serious trouble at Oriental Park once some years ago. He caught a groom abusing a horse and damned near beat him to death. They had to tear him off the guy two or three times."

"I've slugged at least one man for the same reason, Jack. I'd put that on the credit side. He didn't use a weapon, did he?"

"No—but he was mighty tough."

"What about Alonso?"

"Easygoing, sloppy. Not the sort of good-natured goon you'd expect with his indolent way, though. Lonny pays no attention to anything much—gets sudden interests in things and loses them just as fast. Cameras, at one time—had a hell of a siege with sport cars and littered the barn with V-8 engine parts and extra carburetors last year. He's only mildly interested in the horses, although that seems to be his only permanent liking."

"How did he get along with his sister?"

"He paid no attention to her, whatever. Anita always disliked his shiftlessness and he avoided her as much as he could." Jack Ferrier got up again and wandered over to the fireplace—put his glass on the mantel. "Doc, what would you say if we did that?—got everybody together at Cielito—say tomorrow night—and put the whole deal right on the line?"

"No cops?"

"That would be my first guess. No cops."

"Where would it get us?"

Ferrier ducked his head down and scratched his ear—studied the hearth awhile. "Well—it would be a hell of a shock to that smug mob, for one thing. They'd try not to believe it." He looked up quickly. "Unless you declare yourself as only interested because Anita had spoken to you and that you were simply reporting what line the police were going to take—a friendly gesture to me, perhaps."

I weighed that some. I wasn't sure a friendly gesture to Ferrier would get me much co-operation. "I'll go along with you as far as my feeling of responsibility to your wife goes. That's the literal truth. I'd feel a little more sure of myself, though, without friendly gestures to anybody. What would you think if I lay it on the line, as you suggest, but lead them to believe that I have all the facts on the Bolado matter? Carlos may say it's of no interest to him, but it's pretty sure to be of interest to one of them!"

"I'd say you might smoke somebody out—one way or another." Jack Ferrier gave me that tired smile again.

16

THURSDAY EVENING, OCTOBER 11

Perhaps you have noted that I have made no entry in this chronicle for the evening of October 10, Wednesday—last night. It is not that I have nothing to report. Actually, I have a great deal to report. However, the—material—is such that I am determined to set it down with proper restraint and, for once, with some semblance of objectivity. There is quite enough sensationalism in our crime writing as it is. It will be sufficient to say that I set down nothing in this journal at Cielito.

I was otherwise occupied.

Jack Ferrier called one of his brothers-in-law—Juan—from my place before he left on Tuesday night. The others yesterday morning. They all agreed to meet at Cielito by six or earlier yesterday afternoon. Ferrier set me up on the office extension while he talked to Juan so I'd get the guy's attitude . . .

"Johnny?" All very pleasant and up-tempo. It sounded a little phony to me because Ferrier had been pretty down all evening. "This is Jack."

"What's on your mind?"

"There's something come up that makes it damned important that we all get together sometime tomorrow."

"The business? There's not much you can do about that until—"

"Not the business, Johnny. It's more important than the business right now. I'm calling you because you're the one member of the family that can get the rest of them out. Listen, Johnny, the police are getting ready to say that one of us killed Anita!"

"That *what?*" He didn't raise his voice for some reason. "One of us? You mean one of the family?"

"*They* mean one of the family. I don't—necessarily."

"How the hell could they figure that, Jack? It's stupid!" Then, sharply, "What do you mean—*necessarily?*"

"I mean that, unless we head it off some way tomorrow, we'll make every front page in town with the damnedest scandal you ever heard before this thing is over!"

"If Ramon had said that, I'd laugh at him. Coming from you, it scares me, Jack. What sort of scandal? They certainly wouldn't report that they—*suspected* one of us. We could blow the roof off."

"Look; I can't tell you about it over the phone. Can you be at Cielito around six or before tomorrow night?"

"Of course—if it's that bad. How about dropping by for a drink tonight—or can I come over there? Where are you now?"

"I'm at Doc Connor's—"

"What the hell has *he* got to do with it? Don't let that phony get to you, Jack. Did you know he went to Cuba? Is he the one that's—"

"Connor's the one who's trying to get us to straighten the thing out before the police foul us up. He went to Cuba for me. I asked him to go."

"I'll be damned! Listen, Jack, will you drop by on your way home? I'll go off my chump if I don't know more about it!"

So Ferrier spent half an hour with Juan on his way home. That meeting—and conversations with the other brothers yesterday morning—were supposed to take some of the pressure off me at Cielito.

So I left the "No Clinic Today" sign on the office door, figuring I might not be up to it in the morning, and rode out to Tioga Village with Ferrier. We got to the farm about five-thirty. From far across the hill, as we drove up to the door, we could see a man cantering a horse—bright against the late afternoon sun.

Ferrier said, "Johnny's early."

The man gave no sign he'd seen us, but put the big chestnut at a rail-fence panel and eased down the slope toward the barn. A figure in jeans came out of the barn and stood waiting for him.

Two cars were standing in the parking area. We pulled alongside and got out. Ferrier stood for a moment by the car. When I came around he touched my arm—gently restrained me. With his other hand he made a sweeping gesture across the paddocks as though he were calling my attention to the beauty of the place. Juan Angel was just dismounting at the barn.

"Doc, I've been trying to make up my mind all the way out to say something . . ."

"So, Jack? Why not?"

"Carlos is here, too—that's his car. When I talked to him today, he—didn't have the same attitude you saw in Havana." Ferrier glanced up toward the porch and quickly leaned back into the car and pretended to reach for something. Carlos Angel stood in the doorway. "I'll have to make it fast. He's suspicious as hell. Don't talk to him, Doc—I was wrong about him . . ." Angel started down the steps. Ferrier was still fumbling in the glove compartment.

"He's coming down here. Tell me about it—quick!"

"I think he tried to have you killed in Havana—not sure. He just talked that way."

Angel met us at the foot of the steps. He disregarded his brother-in-law. "Good afternoon, Dr. Connor. Am I to understand you're here in some official capacity?"

"I think you know that I have no official capacity whatever, Mr. Angel. I thought you had agreed to hear what I have to say."

"There is no question in my mind, Connor, but that we must hear what you have to say. Since you insist on having something to say—and apparently aren't too particular about where you say it."

Jack Ferrier said, "Wait a minute, Carlos! You know perfectly—"

"I know nothing! I simply want an understanding with this man, Jack. We agree to listen only because we have no choice. I want to tell you to your face, Connor, that your intrusion into our affairs is unpardonable—and unwelcome!" Before I could get the hair down on my scalp again, he'd stalked off down the drive toward the barn.

Ferrier muttered something under his breath and turned back to me. "Come on, Doc. Let's go in."

I said, "Welcome to Hacienda Cielito!"—stared after Carlos Angel. I think I was a little afraid of the nastiness of the man—afraid, particularly, because I knew, then, that he was able to make me lose control of myself. I said, "O.K., Jack. I don't like it, but I asked for it."

"They won't all be that way."

We were met at the door by a tall, bony individual in a black alpaca coat. He looked completely American, but spoke in Spanish, greeting us each by name and taking our coats and hats. We went into the big living room. There was a fire going and drinks had been set out.

I nodded toward the hall. "Old retainer?"

Ferrier grunted. "New retainer. He's worked around the area for years. Ramon hired him seven, eight months ago because he spoke a little Spanish. He used to be a ship steward on a South American run, I think."

"Can you tell me more about Carlos now—the attitude thing?"

"Nothing very direct. The man was extraordinarily vicious when he spoke about your trip south. See if I can quote him: 'From what I hear,' yes, that's the way he put it, 'From what I hear, Connor, with your rum-running pal, Charley Toy, was lucky to get out of Cuba alive'."

"That could mean anything, of course."

"It could, Doc, if Carlos hadn't left Havana several hours before you were attacked." Ferrier raised his head suddenly There was a step in the hall. "Will you have a drink, Doc?"

"Yes, thanks—bourbon, if you will." The long frame of the house man lanked across the hall and disappeared to the other side of the building. "What's he called?"

"Parrish." He raised his voice very slightly and repeated the name. "Parrish."

"Did you call, sir?" The voice and the soft step came from the hall. Parrish appeared at the door.

"I think we'd like some Angostura, please."

As the man walked away, Ferrier said, "He's been briefed, Doc."

"Yeah." Among other things they claim for Angostura is that it settles your stomach. I wasn't in a mood to get professional about it. We'd just poured the drinks when Juan Angel came in—very neat, too, in proper boots and good, worn cord. Worn in the right places. I'd have to watch my own blind spot with this one.

"Hello, Connor." He stood well across the room, which saved him any decision on handshaking. "Jack . . ."

Ferrier said hello and I muttered something. Juan eased over to the table and made himself a drink. Took his time. Then he said, "Just what do you think this—conclave—will accomplish, Doctor?"

"I have no idea, Mr. Angel. I understand Jack, here, went into it pretty fully with you last night."

Ferrier broke in. "Johnny knows some of it, Doc. He doesn't like it much."

"Why the hell should I like it? Even the Tioga police think Connor has no business messing around with the case—"

"Wait a minute, Angel!" I'd have to sell the lot of them anyway, so I might as well start here. "If I had 'messed around,' as you call it, a day or two sooner, your sister might well be living today."

"I don't believe that!" He didn't yell, but he was emphatic enough. "You're both implying that someone on the place attacked her—someone in the family, actually. It's stupid!"

Jack Ferrier said, "Look, Johnny, if the family doesn't listen to Doc Connor, they're going to have to listen to the police—not the Tioga Village police, but the big-time cops from the city. I'm convinced of that." Juan started to say something. Ferrier rode him down. "Use your head. Doc isn't a cop and he isn't stupid. If it was one of us, Johnny, as impossible as it seems, wouldn't you want him—held accountable?"

"I—don't know. Probably not. What good would it do? Who-ever it . . ." He gave it up. "It just couldn't be! Nobody would do that sort of thing again, anyway."

I said, "He did it once before."

Jack Ferrier stood up and set his glass down on the table. "He did do it before, Johnny. I have the proof." The fire went out of him. "Why don't we wait until later for all this?"

Juan Angel finished his drink, his back to us. Then he turned and walked out of the room. Ferrier grunted. "You'll have a rough trip, Doc."

"I dislike to see pleasant people in trouble. He could hardly have any other attitude." I said the words, but I was having a little difficulty with my determination. It wasn't the first time I'd wished I hadn't started something.

"He's honest, Doc." Jack went over to the big window. "The clan is gathering. Here comes Merry—"

"Mariano? The Sanskrit boy?"

"Yes. The youngest. Let's not get cornered here again. We can walk down to my place . . ."

"All right. I'd just as soon not have to go over this one at a time—quite yet, anyway."

We walked out and met young Mariano Angel as he came up the steps. A small, bony man, looking older than his mid-thir-ties, with a black mustache and wet, dark eyes. He offered no greetings. "Ramon said to tell you that there won't be any sit-down dinner. Cook has the stuff to eat and old Parrish will haul it to you wherever you want."

"Thanks, Merry. You know Dr. Connor."

"Yes. How do you do, Doctor. In case anybody's forgotten to say 'welcome,' maybe I'd better."

"Thank you." He seemed quite serious about it, so I didn't crack.

Ferrier laughed abruptly. "Good man, Merry. I hoped some-body would remember his manners."

Mariano opened his dark eyes as though in surprise. "It isn't exactly manners, Jack." He went into the house without expla-nation.

As we walked down the hill toward the barn, I wondered how Ferrier felt about going back to the little house where Anita had died. The lowering sun set the windows ablaze and blinded us as we turned the long curve of the drive. Jack marched sternly on. The place seemed the only escape from the brother-by-brother process I'd been going through and I wondered . . .

"Jack; I realize you're taking me down here to—avoid embarrassment. I hope you don't—"

"Forget it, Doc. The cottage is my home—more so than the apartment could ever have been. I want to keep it that way." He touched my arm very gently. "I'm glad it's you."

"Thanks."

"Anita loved it, too, you know."

We walked on.

One of the shed doors at the end of the barn was open and a man was bending over the engine of a stripped automobile chassis. He looked up as we passed, went back to work without speaking. Ferrier said, "That's Lonny."

At the gate, he paused with his hand on the latch.

"Yes, Doc, Anita loved this house. You know how I know she loved it so much?"

"How, Jack?"

The man turned and looked across toward the barn—to the big sliding door in the center. "See what I mean, Doc? See how far that is? She walked all that way to come home!"

17

Ferrier had sent word to the big house that we wouldn't want dinner brought down and we had made some ham and eggs. Once, while we'd sat talking, the phone had rung and Ramon had sent word that they'd be ready for us at seven-thirty. At twenty-five after, we started walking up the hill. Jack had the Bolado documents in his pocket and, though I had never seen them, I knew they contained nothing but the evidence that one of the Angel family—one of the men—had been with young Bolado the day he disappeared. Ferrier assured me there was no hint of which brother was involved.

It was Ramon, the unctuous, who met us in the hall and gestured us into the big living room with all the impersonal warmth of a professional pallbearer. "The servants have retired to their quarters." With this, he went to a big chair, facing the entire room, and sat down. Jack and I found places together along the irregular circle of men who studiously avoided watching us. Ramon cleared his throat.

"Because this meeting seems unavoidable, gentlemen, I hope we can manage to make it as brief—and painless—as possible. We were called together at the insistence of Jack Ferrier, who apparently feels that we are under suspicion in the tragic death of our sister."

A couple of very nasty sounds came across the room—restrained and unrecognizable, but nasty. The eldest Angel cleared his throat again.

"Don't start that, now! I think we all hold the same feeling of resentment, and most of us have expressed it well enough already. Let's get this over with." He turned to. Ferrier. "Jack, you'd better explain."

Somebody said, "I'll say he'd better!"

Juan Angel said, "Shut up, Lonny!"

Jack Ferrier pulled his envelope from his pocket and re-moved a considerable bundle of papers. He leaned back in his chair and took a long, challenging look around the room.

"Here is a fact with which none of you is familiar. I thought, for a while, it might not be necessary to disclose it. It has now become necessary. About eight weeks ago, a man—unnamed for the moment—came to me and demanded an exorbitant sum of money for what he called 'the facts in the Bolado case.' I looked at what he had to offer—and paid him."

The room broke out angrily. *"What?"* Carlos Angel was on his feet. "You mean to say you actually paid some blackmailer for so-called facts in—"

"I mean exactly that, Carlos."

More exclamations from the room. Ferrier said, "Let me get on with this. What's the use of yelling about it until you know what the man had dug up?"

"That's right." Ramon thumped on the arm of his chair. "We'll get no place this way. I don't believe a damned word of it, but I want to hear what he has to say. Now shut up, will you?"

"Thanks, Carlos." Ferrier opened the documents and put on a pair of glasses—tortoise-rimmed things I'd never seen him wear before. "I have the so-called facts here, gentlemen. The first one is a deposition from the Bolado boy's father. Any of you who wish may read it in detail later. It seems suffi-cient, now, to say that on October sixth, 1931, he states, young Caesar, known simply as Bolado around the waterfront, left home in the morning to pick up and deliver a grocery order to the freight boat, *Cisne*. He had been promised fifty cents for the job, American. The father did not know from which store the groceries were purchased, nor who had originally ordered them. It was the last time he saw his son until he was called to identify the body."

Juan called across the room. "Who ordered the stuff? You, Jack?"

"No. I never bought groceries on the Havana side if I could help it—then only provisions in such quantities as we'd load at the dock, certainly not by tender. I don't know who ordered them. I do know, though, that they were delivered."

"Why hasn't all this come out?" I looked across and saw Alonso barking at everybody in general. "The police made a thorough investigation at the time."

Ferrier held up his hand. "Give me a chance. I can tell you, now, however, that I'm not the first one of the family to be blackmailed."

"Who, then?" Carlos, for some reason, was in a particular rage. "Why haven't we known about it?"

"Anita's been blackmailed—for more than twenty years—do you hear *that?* For more than twenty years my wife—your sister—has been protecting one of you from—prosecution!"

Carlos sank back in his chair. Ramon said, "Go on, Jack."

Ferrier calmed down and looked back at his papers. "Then follows a deposition by Estella Monterez—*nana*. In part, it reads, 'On the day of the disappearance of Caesar Bolado Vega, I was engaged in housework in the living room of the house. Miss Anita Angel was in her room on the third floor. Both rooms overlook the water and the desolate stretch of beach where Jack Ferrier's boat, *Cisne,* was moored. At about one-thirty in the afternoon—'"

Ramon said, *"Nana* never wrote that!"

"Of course she didn't!" Ferrier was brusque. "It was written for her—in Spanish, by the way—read to her, signed by her, and witnessed by Caesar Bolado Vega's father—old Caesar. They witnessed each other's statements, our blackmailer's little device for keeping his secrets intact."

Lonny said, "I'm not sure that's legal."

"What's that got to do with it, Lonny?" Mariano's voice was laconic. "Nobody's being tried, either, but I'd hate like hell to see it in the *Times!*"

Jack started reading again, "'At about one-thirty in the afternoon of October sixth, I looked out and saw the tender being rowed out to the *Cisne*. I recognized the young Bolado at the oars. He was wearing an old red cotton shirt in which I had seen him many times before and the officer's cap which I knew Jack Ferrier had given him. There was a large box on the stern seat of the tender. I knew Captain Ferrier did not wish unauthorized persons to come aboard his boat, so I went to the front part of the house where an extra key was kept which would let the family into the boat. There was also a key to the engine. These were in the hall-table drawer where they belonged, so I felt the lad could do no great harm and went back to my work, looking out occasionally at the *Cisne*. After perhaps fifteen or twenty minutes, when the tender had not returned, I was somewhat concerned and kept a closer watch. It was then I saw someone swimming toward the boat. When he got to the side, young Bolado reached down and helped him aboard. Although I had not heard anyone come in through the front door, I went again to the hall and, this time, found the keys gone. I was relieved to know that one of the family had gone aboard. I did not pay much attention to the boat after that, but became busy in other parts of the house. At dinner, when I heard the boys relating where they had been and none of them spoke of having been at the boat, I thought, perhaps, it had been some youthful prank, but before speaking of the possibility that a stranger might have taken the keys, which had been replaced before dinner time, I searched for and found the wet bathing suit.'"

Jack Ferrier paused in his reading. This time there was not a sound in the room but the movement of the men in their chairs as they turned to look at one another.

Ramon said quietly, "She must have recognized the suit."

Ferrier ignored this. "She goes on, 'The bathing suit was in the little bathhouse back of the kitchen. It had been hidden. Since all the boys were fully dressed when they returned to the house, I judge the swimmer had changed his clothes there. It was not until I heard of the death of young Bolado that I spoke to Miss Anita about what I had seen. We agreed to say nothing of the matter to anyone. I have not done so until now, when I make these statements, at her request and through her representative.'"

Somebody said, *"Her* representative!"

Carlos said, "Yes. What was *that* for?"

Ferrier folded the papers and carefully replaced them in his pocket. He took his glasses off. "The man was careful, in the depositions, not to use the word 'attorney,' although he represented himself as Anita's lawyer to *nana.*"

Ramon spoke again. "Jack; I suggested before that *nana* must have recognized the suit."

"She did, Ramon."

The big, oily man thought it over. "Then she would have told Anita?"

"Yes. She would have told Anita."

"And you say Anita was blackmailed?"

"I suppose you couldn't call it blackmail. There were no threats." Ferrier sank back in his chair and dropped his head. Sighed. "Anita has paid old Caesar more than five thousand dollars in twenty years."

Carlos became immediately alert. "But that's ridiculous, Jack! Surely the fact that one of us was—might have been— along with the Bolado boy when the accident occurred wouldn't have ruined him for life. Why wasn't it discussed openly?"

"If you will remember, Carlos, there didn't seem to be any need for such a discussion. The police inquiries were most casual and the matter was dropped almost immediately."

Carlos pursued the question. "The matter was dropped and no criminal—or even neglectful—action was ever attributed to anybody concerned. Even if our sister felt it should be hushed up, why the hell would *you* fall for a blackmailer? I take it for granted you don't want to tell us who he is—this extortionist."

"That's right." Ferrier still sat as though exhausted.

Alonso moved abruptly in his chair. "The thing I can't understand is what all this wash has to do with Anita's death. Has Doc Connor got some theory about that?"

I said, "Yes. I have a theory. I'll tell you about it when Jack is finished."

"I still want to know," Carlos looked at his cigar butt and threw it away, "why you'd let yourself be pushed around by a blackmailer, Jack."

"It may not be understandable to you, Carlos—or any of you, for that matter—but when I learned that Anita had known about the Bolado affair all along and said nothing—well—that was good enough for me. We have never discussed it—before or since."

Juan said, "All right. So Jack paid off the guy. That's his business. What's this theory of Doc Connor's that ties the accident up with Anita's death?"

Ferrier shook his head and sat up slowly. I was going to say something and held it. The gray man made his familiar gesture of distress—knuckled his head with his big fist. "It wasn't an accident, Johnny."

They believed him. There was a stiff, hard silence in the room for a moment until they realized that no one wanted to believe him. Then they started to exclaim. I watched faces—could read nothing from them that didn't belong there. Little Willie, hiding somewhere in the room, was cowering behind a changing mask of indignation, surprise, curiosity—or what? They all looked pretty much as anybody would have looked under the circumstances. For once the eldest, Ramon, was unable to cope with the group. It took Juan to shout them down and be heard. His face was drawn and pale. I don't know whether he was angry or afraid. His voice was low, tense.

"You'd better make it stick, Jack. That's a damned serious accusation."

Ferrier looked around the circle of hostile faces. "I knew it was—not an accident—the afternoon it happened. It seems that, now, we have come to the point of the meeting. The Bolado boy was beaten to death with a gaff handle. I washed the blood off it and put it away when I came aboard."

The only sound in the room was a whispered, "Why?"

Jack looked at Merry Angel. "Because I was engaged to your sister. Because I was on my way to Miami and didn't hear of the boy's death until I got back. Because shortly after that it was declared an accident. That's why. That's why I threw the boy's cap overside, too." He studied the faces before him for a moment. "Perhaps now you'll understand why I tried to protect Anita from this—to protect all of us. Yet Anita's life was destroyed in exactly the *same terrible way* a little more than a week ago. Do you understand, now? *Do* you? Do you, Carlos?—Ramon?—Johnny? . . ." His voice fell away. I spoke.

"Take it easy, Jack. There's a long way to go."

Juan made a sudden, impatient gesture with his hand. "All right, Connor, let's have the rest of it!"

Carlos, still furious, shouted, "To hell with Connor! Jack Ferrier talks about *his* being blackmailed! We're the ones who are being blackmailed! I, for one, wouldn't hesitate for a moment to turn this phony over to the police right now."

Nobody brandished anything in resentful fervor and Carlos sat back in his chair huffing and puffing. Young Mariano's quiet drawl cut clearly across the muttering. "If Doc Connor's a blackmailer, why don't we wait until he sets a price on his information. Then you can take him to the cops—personally—Carlos. Go ahead, Doc."

I took a big breath and plunged in. "Mariano Angel is right. When and if I offer you any escape whatever from the responsibilities of this inquiry, you can take me to the police. Until then, it's my purpose to take *one of you* to the police."

A stormy wave of growls came up and Juan said, "That's tough talk, mister."

I barked, I think. "Of course it's tough talk. Listen to me, now. A week ago Tuesday evening, Anita Ferrier knew that the old Bolado affair had come back to taunt at least three persons in this family. She knew her husband was being threatened, she knew who had gathered the information with which he was being threatened, and she knew which one of you had killed the boy, Bolado."

"You're taking a lot for granted, Connor!" It was Ramon.

"I am taking almost nothing for granted. On October sixth, nineteen thirty-one, the boy was beaten to death with a gaff handle. An exhumation would permit a more careful examination of the skull and show patterned fractures which could not have been made by rocky ledges. Bolado was murdered—possibly under extreme provocation—possibly even in self-defense. I don't know. I do know, however, that a member of this family was with him at the time.

"Anita Ferrier knew this and asked me to help her. If she had been completely frank with me that night, I might have saved her life. If her murderer had held off one more day and she had kept her appointment with me on Wednesday morning, I could have saved her life. Then Jack Ferrier came to me and I agreed to do what I could to help. That is what I am doing here to-night—trying to help Jack Ferrier and the four of you who are unwittingly harboring a dangerous psychopathic."

Ramon spoke again, ponderously, this time, to cover the agitation which was so obvious in his every physical movement. "Your ideas, Connor, seem psychopathic in themselves. I do not have to be an attorney to remind you that your statements are libelous in the extreme. Nor do I need to be an attorney to remind you, as well, that—no matter what may have happened in 1931—you have shown us nothing whatever to suggest that any member of this family had anything to do with the death of our sister."

I sensed a quality of desperation in the room. I think my unfounded faith in the exhumation had presented a shocking picture to each of the brothers—of dreadful scandal to four of them and of death, possibly, to the fifth. If I wanted tension, I was getting it. When Ramon finished speaking, the group remained completely quiet. A car passed on the road below and each man in the room, for his own reasons, was wondering if it would turn in. It had gone into the distance before I spoke again.

"You are quite right, Mr. Angel. I have shown no connection between the—actions—except their similarity. Except their similarity and, of course, the motive and opportunity for the second one. You need not be a lawyer, either, to understand that, when the killer of Bolado is named, the investigation of Anita Ferrier's death will take on an entirely new aspect."

"Named?" Alonso was almost shouting this time. "What do you mean?"

I deliberately sidestepped. "I mean that the police, then, will have a specific target for their investigation—an individual —a suspect. They will re-examine and recheck his alibis. They will direct the attention of the police laboratories to his clothing, his person, the pattern of his pores, his—"

Carlos interrupted savagely. "My brother asked you a direct question. I want it answered. What do you mean when you so confidently say that Bolado's killer will be *named?* Your whole premise has been callously and unfairly based on what you claim was known to two women who were very dear to us all—and who are now dead. What do you mean by such a statement, Connor?"

Ferrier gave me a quick, taut look—pressed my elbow with his in sudden warning. I had a bitter temptation to bait the trap with Buzz Chapin's worthless hide. But not me! Not good ol' Doc! This one I knew was loaded, but I heard my cue and made a grandstand, if ill-advised, entrance.

"Mr. Angel, I believe you told me, in Havana, that you had talked to *nana,* Estella Monterez, just before her death?"

Carlos snapped, "That is correct."

"Did she tell you whether she had disclosed the name of Bolado's—companion—to me?"

"She told me she had not—that is—"

"You asked her about it specifically?"

He was angry, fumbling. "Certainly. I knew you were investigating the matter."

"How did you know, Mr. Angel?"

"That is a family affair and none of your damned business!"

I took it easily so he wouldn't holler again, said, "It very possibly is none of my business, as you say. Can you think of any reason, Mr. Angel, why, if she *had* disclosed the name to me, she would not have admitted it, say, to *you?*"

"Why!" He really blew up at that. "You've practically accused me of—"

Mariano broke in—sounded almost as if he were amused. "Wait a minute, Carlos! You're yapping yourself into a hole!" He twisted back in his chair to face me. "Look, Connor; this

is damned serious business and I think it probably should be
looked into. But I believe we should have the right to get ourselves straightened out on it first. I think we've got to fight it
out among ourselves or we'll be at a rotten disadvantage with—
well—publicity and all that. Don't you agree that we should
have that chance?"

"That's why I'm here tonight, Merry, instead of the police.
I have said nothing to anyone. I want you especially to know
that I have not even taken Jack Ferrier into my complete confidence—nor will I share it with you until you are ready, as a
group, to act properly on it."

Ramon spoke from his big chair. "I am inclined to agree
with Merry—regardless of the merits of Connor's case. As I
have said previously, we have no choice." He cleared his throat
ponderously. "I wish to ask the doctor a straight question, however, and I want a straight answer."

"Very well."

"Are you implying to us that *nana* Monterez disclosed to you
the identity of—Bolado's companion, as you call him?"

"That is *exactly* what I am implying, Mr. Angel."

18

From here in, the dates on which I set down the chapters of this narrative lose any significance. I need only to tell you what happened during the remainder of Wednesday night and my part in the life of Little Willie Angel will have been played. In the long, precise processes of the law which will inch him toward his ultimate destruction, I have no interest.

Shall we go back to the point where Jack Ferrier and I left the band of demoralized Angels behind us and walked through the early night toward the cottage? There seemed to be a good deal to think about at the time, and neither of us had spoken until we'd almost reached the barn. Then Ferrier said, "Now what, Doc?"

"Now, I think, you make some excuse to go back and join the argument. I'll stay here at the cottage until you're free to drive me to town."

"I can't leave you alone here. That's going really too far with it, Doc."

I'd already gone too far with it; for my dough. "I'd rather have you up there counting noses, Jack. They're convinced, I think, that you don't know any more than you've told the family. Go back up and keep tabs on them."

He shrugged. "All right. I hope to hell you know what you're doing. You really asked for it up there."

We walked into the living room. Ferrier closed his eyes once, hard, as he turned toward the bitter image he must have seen in front of the fireplace. He swung back and faced me again.

"You want a gun?"

"I suppose so. Have you got one?"

He opened the lid of a window seat and dug under some blankets. "Here. It's a target job, but it's the best I can do." He handed me a beautiful Woodsman—too long and light for close work. "Stick it somewhere you can get at it. It's loaded."

I pushed the gun down behind the cushions of the couch. "Is this telephone on the house line?"

Ferrier came over and flipped a switch. "Like that it is. When it's down—like this—there's a direct trunk outside. The only extension on that line is in the tack room at the barn."

"But when the thing is up, it's tied in with all the extensions at the main house?"

"That's right—and there are three or four of them up there." He thought a moment. "Four, Doc. One downstairs in the front hall, one in the upstairs hall, and one in the kitchen. The other one goes to the servants' house, but can be cut off."

"Right. Jack, get up there, now, and see what goes on. They're bound to come up with some sort of a plan and you'll have to string along with them. But keep 'em stirred up. Somebody's got to lose his head."

He started off—looked back from the door. "For God's sake, Doc, take care of yourself, will you?"

"You're reading my mind, pal. Don't worry."

"O.K." He smiled and went out.

I pulled the gun out and checked it again—dumped the load and rehearsed the action and safety until it felt natural. Then I hid it again in the couch. I couldn't see Little Willie coming after me with a gun. Not unless things had closed in on him so tightly that he knew he had no chance. All he had to do, as it was, was to sit tight and invite us to prove things.

But Little Willie was unpredictable.

I looked at my watch. It was only a few minutes past nine. From the picture window I could see a considerable area which was marked out by the room lights. It occurred to me that, if I turned on most of the downstairs lights, I'd be able to see anyone approaching the house. I walked through to the kitchen and turned on a porch light which I found. It illuminated most of the back and one side of the cottage. A dining-room fixture did the rest.

I went out and stood in the area between the barn and the house. No one could possibly approach the place without being seen. Even though the autumn night had not completely settled, I knew I could station myself, later, at some point away from the house and be sure nobody sneaked in. The big central door to the barn was open and I wandered into the building. The light from the front windows of the cottage showed me, dimly, that the tack room faced the doorway. There would be a flashlight somewhere among the tack and I'd forgotten to ask Jack Ferrier for one.

For a few moments I stood in the tack-room doorway and listened to the pleasant small sounds around me—the steady crunching of grain from the stall of some late feeder—the gentle blowing of a nose—the earthy thud of a foot where a fussy fellow had pawed away his bedding.

I wondered, vaguely, how these horses had accepted the frightful, bloody doings which had invaded their quiet home the week before. Horses become quickly aware of violence, even when carried to them only in small sounds and scents.

I found my flashlight easily enough—a long, heavy, Navy-surplus thousand-footer that suggested its worth at once as a weapon when I picked it up. Shielding the big glare under my coat, I took a look around. The telephone extension was on a narrow shelf that ran the length of the room. There was a comfortable chair facing the screened door from which, I discovered, I could command a perfect view of the lighted areas around the cottage—areas through which any approach from the main house seemed at all feasible. Then, too, I had the telephone.

I went back to the Ferrier place convinced I'd be wise to retreat to the tack room if I sensed any danger in remaining at the cottage. How I was going to sense any more danger than was already squirming at my back doesn't seem to have occurred to me.

At the foot of the stairway I noticed a draft from the second floor and went up to investigate. There was an open window in the front bedroom—apparently shared, in happier days, by the Ferriers. Anita's gowns still hung in the closet and a handsome photograph of her stood, silver-framed, on the highboy.

I left the lights burning in the bedroom and made the rounds of the house, locking windows. The kitchen door I bolted.

Then the telephone rang.

I picked up the instrument. It felt like a grenade with the pin out. Jack Ferrier spoke urgently. "Get this situation. I may have to hang up fast, but I can see all of them from where I am in the hall." He paused. "You there?"

"Right. Go ahead."

"I had to tell them about Chapin, Doc, I *had* to—"

"Oh no, Jack! You'll blow the whole thing. You say you've told them?"

"Yes. They were coming down after you in a body, goddammit, Doc! They wanted to lock you up until they got our attorney here. That would have blown the whole thing, for sure. I had to take the pressure off you, someway—"

"Who proposed locking me up?"

"I don't know who started it."

"Anybody object—beside you?"

"Johnny."

"How about Mariano?"

"He was all for it. He and Ramon."

"Carlos?"

"Carlos went for the Chapin thing immediately. He forgot all about you the minute I mentioned it. He's making a big speech in there now about what we ought to do to Chapin."

"Hell, Jack, I might as well go home!"

"As far as anybody's jumping you is concerned, maybe, but this meeting is about to explode. Stick around. I need you." He sounded as if he might need somebody, at that. "Doc; I'm not sure they'd let either of us leave—hold it!—may call later."

And that was that. It was not more than two minutes later that I was dumped out of my sulking by another ring. I grabbed the phone and heard Ferrier say, "Heads up! *I can't find Merry!* Watch it!" That was all.

I grabbed the gun from the couch, stuffed it into my belt, and beat it for the outside—put the cottage between me and the big house and did a fast circle to the darkness of the barn door. It was then I realized, for the first time, that the glare from the Ferrier place did me as much harm as good. I couldn't see beyond it.

But I could hear. Somebody stumbled and cursed softly not fifty yards from me—he was evidently coming down the hillside beyond the cottage. I didn't like the feel of the barn at my back and moved off to the end farthest from the sound. There I crouched and waited. The gun poked uncomfortably at my belly, so I held it in my hand. I'd have traded it for the big flashlight in the tack room.

"Connor."

The voice came from somewhere to my left—in the shadows beyond the lighted ground in front of the house. I waited to see if he would show himself.

"Connor!" His voice was still low. "Are you in there, Doc?"

Then I saw him. He was standing at the edge of the shadow looking up at the open front door. I called back softly, "Merry?"

"Yes. How did you know? Where are you?"

"Stand right where you are, Merry. I'm coming over to you. Just don't do any jumping around."

"What happened? Why all the—"

"Take it easy. Nothing happened." I watched him carefully as I walked along the barn toward him. "I didn't expect you, Merry. I thought it might be—one of the others."

That's the way I'd planned to play it—no matter who came.

He said, "One of the others?" His voice was young. Sincere. Puzzled. Then, "*Which* one, Doc?"

I stood a few feet off from him. "Don't you know, Merry? You are the one member of the family I thought might."

"Why, Doc?" Whispered.

"You were fifteen then, weren't you, Merry?" I didn't ask it. I just said it.

"Yeah. I was fifteen." He remembered a moment. "Why did you think I'd know, Doc?"

"How did you get along with your brothers when you were fifteen, Merry?"

"They pushed me around pretty much. I didn't get along with them very well. I don't now, for that matter . . ."

"And—*Anita?*"

He made a simple gesture with his hand. "Listen, Doc. You can forget all that—with me, at least. I'm not the one you're looking for. I sneaked down here to ask you one, simple question. I think you've answered it already."

From the house on the hill came a sharp call. "Merry! Where are you, Merry?"

The little man jumped. "I've got to go. That's Carlos. He'll raise hell if he catches me down here." He took off—sprinted through the barnyard and off to the left of the house. In a few seconds the voice from the hill called again and, this time, Merry answered.

"Yo, Carlos! What do you want?"

He must have shouted away from us—bounced his voice off the opposite hill. He sounded a mile away.

Carlos shouted angrily. "Come back to the house at once! You're wanted here."

Again Merry's distant voice, "I've had enough of that rat race. I'm taking a walk." He even made it sound sullen. Then, "O.K., Carlos, I'm on my way."

I stayed in the shadow and tried to locate him before I moved again. He'd sounded convincing enough—but why not? I was watching the lights of the big house, hoping to catch his silhouette, when he spoke to me from ten feet away.

"I just wanted to ask you if you really believe all that stuff you and Jack cooked up." He laughed unpleasantly. "I mean—is it hypothetical? Maybe something this ass Chapin's got you sold on?"

"Is that what they think up there, Merry?"

"Yes. They were all for locking you up and calling a lot of lawyers until Jack told us it was Buzz. I thought locking you up was a hell of an idea. You'd have been safe, anyway—"

"Safe, Merry? From whom—Buzz Chapin?"

"From—there it is, isn't it! It can't be true—yet, somehow, it *might* be true. You can see how relieved everybody was to find as silly a guy as Buzzy mixed up in it!"

"It is true, Merry. It couldn't have been any other way."

"Bolado—or Anita?" He said it thoughtfully.

"Both, I think—one because of the other."

He hesitated a moment. "It's pretty awful, Doc. I'll do what I can."

"O.K., Merry—but keep your mouth shut and don't take any chances."

"Is it that bad?"

"You saw your sister . . ."

He turned and walked away from me. I heard his quick stride across the paved area—then heard him break into a plugging jog trot as he climbed toward the house on the hill. I knew I hadn't handled him right, but I didn't know why. I was exactly where I'd been before he had sneaked down the hill—only to find me outside instead of securely napping in the comfortable living room.

He had taken a lot of trouble to make character with me. He had also learned—if he was the man I was looking for—that I hadn't the slightest idea what I was talking about. At least that was something he wouldn't be telling his brothers!

I was trying to make some sense out of it when the telephone rang again. This time I heard it both from the cottage and, louder, from the tack room behind me. I groped in and answered it there.

"Dr. Connor? This is Carlos Angel. Is my brother Mariano there with you?"

"No. I heard him shouting to someone up there a minute or two ago. He sounded as though he were on his way back to the—"

"Wait a second, Doctor." His voice faded. "What's that? Oh. All right. Good." Then he was back again. "He's apparently just come in the door. Tell me; are you intending to stay the night?"

"I hadn't thought of it, Mr. Angel. Why?"

"Jack Ferrier feels that you should and I'm inclined to agree with him. We're taking positive action as a family on this thing and I, for one, feel that we should be allowed a little time to investigate it fully before anyone's—overzealousness—makes it a matter of public attention." Pompously reasonable.

"You've seemed unwilling to recognize that I had just that in mind when I came here tonight." I tried to sound a little hurt.

"I know nothing of your motives in coming here, Doctor. You've made a terrible mess of things and I intend to see that you don't make them worse—"

"I intend to see them through, too, Angel. But I also recognize, as I've tried to tell you, that it's a very unhappy situation for all of you—and I have no objection to your investigating it as thoroughly as you wish—as thoroughly as I have." Then I added. "Please tell Jack that I'll be here as long as he wishes me to stay."

"Thank you." He relaxed a little, I thought. "Ferrier has finally admitted the name of the man who apparently bullied him out of several thousand dollars." He must have thought it funny because he made noises of some sort. "It turns out to be a young smart aleck who owes a great deal to this family in one way or another. I think we'll know a lot more about all these so-called documents and charges before we get through with him tonight."

"Tonight?" I hoped against hope that Eddie hadn't broken loose and dragged Chapin to Cielito. "Is Chapin up there now?"

"So you know who he is, Connor! No, he's not here now, Doctor, but he will be here. I have been delegated by the family to bring him out here by the scruff of his scrawny little neck!"

I said "good hunting" or something and uttered a silent, not very sincere prayer for Buzzy. If I knew Carlos—and his attitude toward people who get family money, even Ferrier's, for nothing—the two-hundred-dollar suit was in for a rough night.

As I walked back toward the cottage, someone was coming down the road whistling something, dully. I stood in my tracks until Jack Ferrier turned up.

"Did Carlos tell you what the plan is now?"

"Yeah. Want to go in the house?"

"No. I can't stay. You haven't given up, have you?" He seemed excited. "Lord, Doc! They're wound up tighter than a three-dollar watch. I think most of them are convinced and don't dare admit it. Somebody's going to blow. I know 'em, Doc. Somebody's going to blow!" He rubbed his hand through his hair. "God, I'm tired!"

"You got a drink in the cottage? Might do you good."

"I don't dare, Doc. I'm nervous as hell. I've got to get up there and keep track of them. I won't call back unless somebody's missing. I don't think anybody will move until Carlos starts for town. There's some bourbon in the kitchen cabinet. Help yourself."

Then he was off. I stood there and watched him up the hill against the porch lights of the big house. When he got there, he stood on the porch and lit a cigarette. He was sitting on the railing, smoking, when someone came out, spoke to him briefly, and went down the steps into the darkness.

I saw the taillight of a car go on and heard the motor start—watched the headlights down the road. Carlos would be off after Chapin. I wondered, momentarily, if I'd paid enough attention to Chapin—and certain of his peculiarities. The implications of the Bolado murder were such that . . .

Maybe I hadn't given enough thought to Buzzy at that!

The tack room seemed the best place to sit it out. I disagreed, somewhat, with Jack Ferrier. I felt that, as long as there was some chance of doing something about Chapin and . . .

If Chapin could be taken out of the picture—either by physical threat or violence—and Ferrier's documents disposed of, I'd be out on a limb. I called the house from the tack room—it took some fumbling around, but there was a button there.

"This is Doc Connor. I'd like to speak to Jack Ferrier." I think it was Ramon. "Ferrier? Well, let me see . . ." He faded off the phone and I heard somebody say, "Why not?" Then he hollered for Jack. I waited for an extension to click on. It did and, of course, nobody spoke. He just breathed heavily. The fat Ramon had apparently run up the stairs. I was tempted to give him a clinical cuffola.

"Yes, Doc?"

"Mr. Carlos Angel told me over the telephone that he was going to pick up Buzz Chapin. I promised him I'd stick around as long as you fellows wanted me to."

He didn't sound too puzzled at the repetition. "That's good of you, Doc. We all feel that we may get somewhere with Chapin if we face him down. You realize you pulled a fast one on me tonight when you started talking about naming names. I can't believe that's true, Doc. I think you would have told me."

"Have it your own way, Jack. There's one man up there who knows it's true. Tell him what *nana* said about him. Tell him she said, 'He is as a beautiful child among them. They would turn on him and devour him.' Ask him who *nana* thought was the 'beautiful child among them'?"

"You're overboard, Doc. We can't afford to go overboard. Ramon and Carlos are right. We've got to know where we stand. It's just possible Buzz Chapin's stuff isn't worth anything—that I was rooked. We'll know more about it in a few hours. Take it easy, will you?"

"O.K., I just wanted to be sure you weren't taking a beating, up there. I see you're not. I was afraid they might talk you out of the affidavits. The way you feel now, it doesn't seem to make much difference."

I said it as if I were sore and hung up. They really must have worked on the guy—or he must have worked on them. I was a little disturbed. Ferrier hadn't sounded quite as phony as he should have. I sat back in the big tack-room chair and worried.

Then I *really* worried.

I heard a hinge squeak behind me. At least it sounded like a hinge. It could have been a horse leaning over his half door. I tried not to sell myself the idea it was a horse. I hadn't heard the sound before. I listened with everything—

heard nothing. I found my hand still sweating on the telephone instrument.

They had *called* Jack to the phone—maybe they'd *brought* him to the phone from wherever they had him locked in. There were at least two of the brothers—Ramon and the guy who'd spoken near by—who were out of Ferrier's sight when I'd called. They could have all been out of his sight. The man I hoped was not in the barn at my back could be any of them. Any except Ramon.

I couldn't remember hearing Ramon's wheezing at any time after I'd started talking to Ferrier. But if it was Ramon and he'd run down that fast, I'd hear him wheezing now. Leaving Ramon out, Johnny, Alonso, and Merry—Johnny, Alonso, and Merry—Carlos, too, if he'd . . .

The *hinge* squeaked again.

I untied my shoes and took them off—set them soundlessly aside where I wouldn't kick them. There had been at least two minutes between the squeaks. I ticked the next two minutes off mentally and the third sound came almost on the button. It was no horse.

It was Little Willie . . .

19

I had to make up my mind whether he was looking for me at the cottage—or if he knew where I was. The cautious timing of his approach suggested that he must have heard me on the telephone. I decided he knew I was in the barn and started a cautious advance out of the tack room—groping with each foot before I put it down to avoid stepping on things.

It was past time for the hinge to squeak again, so I had to take it for granted that the man would be well into the barn by this time. My hand touched the screen and I waited there a moment-listening. Somewhere in the far part of the building one of the horses moved quickly—blew out his breath in alarm. The others stopped chewing to listen, then resumed their small, quiet sounds.

They would have done exactly that if a night-foraging rat had moved along the aisle between the stalls, nibbling at scattered grain. Or dragging off such a prize as a silken nest-liner soaked with blood.

I put a gentle pressure against the screen. It yielded an inch with no sound. Then I opened it enough to let me slide through. I made some minor scraping noises getting out, but I'd decided the guy knew where I was, so it wouldn't make too much difference.

Sooner or later he had to know where I was, anyway. It was easy to forget that I was chasing him. Not the other way around. The big open door in front of me was a hell of an invitation to run. It was also, I noted, a hell of an invitation for the man in the dark to pot me. The moon was coming up behind the big house and to my eyes, accommodated to the blackness of the tack room, the yard looked like Broadway. I slipped along the inner wall, wishing I'd taken the trouble to study the place more thoroughly.

A strong, bready odor told me I was near the feed room. I waited there and listened. Both the long-barreled gun and the big flashlight were stuffed into my belt. They were awkward and uncomfortable. I decided to make my stand there—where I'd see the man if he passed in front of the door. If he approached from my rear, I could step into the feed room—or run outside into the nice, open world.

I crouched against the outside wall and put the gun on the concrete sill. The flashlight I held in my hand. There were windows over my head showing a vague light from the outside. I would not stand unless I had to. I waited, listened. Watched the area in front of the door—blinking my eyes occasionally to avoid seeing things that weren't there. My rear I probed with the radar of my crawling ganglia.

I was a very scared guy.

Then, little by little, a chunk of shadow began to detach itself from the dark mass beyond the door. I turned off my spinal radar, but I was getting enough emanations from straight ahead to make up for it.

The man was stooping, close to the inner wall, moving toward the tack-room door. If I'd have been smart, I'd have known he'd approach from that direction. The screen opened that way—away from him as he came up to it. He stopped at the edge of the door. Stood there. I suppose he was listening. I would have been.

I said, "You looking for somebody?"

I could sense his stiffening surprise to hear my voice coming from a distance away from the tack room. He stepped quickly back into the shadow without speaking. I gave him a chance to collect himself before I said anything again.

"I'm right here, Angel."

Then he spoke. The voice was just beyond a whisper—but its throaty quality shook me to my toes . . .

"You have made a great deal of trouble for me, Doctor."

It was the voice of Anita Ferrier! Maybe it was deeper in pitch—it must have been, I suppose. Perhaps it was a little sharper, too, and more pettish than hers would ever have been. But that's in retrospect. That's now—not then. There, in the darkness, it was her own husky contralto come to life. I needed to hear it again . . .

"You have made a great deal of trouble for yourself." I kept it as level as I could. "Do you feel like telling me about it?"

"You, Doctor? Why should I tell you about anything?"

"I might be able to help you, some way."

He laughed softly. I guess it was a laugh. "Everybody is so good to me! I can hardly bear it." There was an element of vicious pride in the vocal masquerade. "Now you! It's too wonderful!"

"Your sister tried to help you for years—protected you, Angel."

"Very lofty of her, too, poor dear. What a pity some beast struck her down!" His body showed again in the dimness.

"You wouldn't have become angry with her and done it yourself, would you, Angel?"

His bulk was moving slowly and steadily toward me. "Of *course* not! She was very dear to me. You didn't think I'd come down here to confess killing my sister, did you?"

"No—frankly. I thought you were coming down here to eliminate the only person left in the world who knows who you are." His moving shadow made it very difficult for me to keep my mind on the business of goading him.

"That's absurd! Why would I *kill* anybody?"

"Want me to tell you why?" He was still about twenty feet away as he moved into the near shadow and I lost him. I rejected the idea of using the flashlight to see if he had a gun in his hand.

"It would be *most* interesting, Doctor."

"You would kill anyone who knew—and rejected—your real self, Angel." I searched frantically for him. Tried to listen. Waited.

"Goody! Tell me about my real self." He seemed no closer.

"You showed it to the Bolado boy—and were rejected. Your sister found it out and rejected you." I could hear his breathing, then—irregular, angry. "And Angel . . ."

"What?"

He sounded very close, then. I clutched my big flashlight, held it at waist level and out from my body. "Why were you—cast off—by Buzzy Chapin?"

I heard him gasp sharply—close up. Maybe ten feet from me. I think he must have frozen in his tracks. He didn't speak for a time. I gave him another dig . . .

"After you'd told him all about—"

He cut me off. His voice was soft, but shaking with an on-rushing hysteria he couldn't handle.

"Oh—you—*bastard!* You—*dirty—rotten—bastard!*" Every word carried him to a new peak, a new, high-pitched sound which would be a screech. *"So you and Ferrier bought him out! Bought him out! God damn you, I'll tear you apart! I'll . . ."*

He did screech as he charged me—a dreadful scream that startled every living thing in that great barn into violent protest. I heard a man's voice shouting somewhere near as he hit, knee up, and knocked me back. I fell and he rolled onto me, one hand clutching at my hair, the other scratching my cheek—deep and hard.

I tried to punch him in the belly, but was too close. His threshing leg hit the flashlight and knocked it away. I got hold of his collar and pulled his head sidewise. He bit my arm. He kept screaming, but I could hear someone shouting, "Doc! Doc, where are you?"

I pulled an arm free and slapped out with it—caught him full in the face. He was strong. His snarling breath had whisky on it. I lost my hold of his collar and he made it to his feet, dragging me up with him. I grabbed for his arm, missed it, and took a hard blow on the wrist from something solid and heavy. He tried to raise it high enough to hit me on the head. My hand slid along its wooden surface—came up against its rope loop. A twitch again!

Somebody was pounding along toward us—shouting. The body in my arms twisted violently away—was free for a moment, and the club smashed down on my shoulder. I pushed him away with my free hand, but he spun fast and I ducked down in time to avoid the blow that followed.

I was trying to get up when something heavy hit me from behind and knocked me down again. I heard a man yell, "Doc—it's me—Ferrier!" He fell across me . . .

I felt the guy swinging the club again as his legs pressed against my shoulder. There was a dreadful hollow thud above me—then another and another. I locked my arms around the legs and pulled. The man went down as Ferrier's weight slumped off my back.

Someone else yelled and a flashlight beam played on us. I drove my right into the soft belly beneath me. The man dropped his club, retching and gasping for air.

The lights in the barn went on. I pulled myself to my feet as Johnny Angel ran up.

He said, "Connor! What the . . . good God!"

I said, "Grab that guy before he gets away." Then I saw Jack Ferrier. He was lying on his side, his knees pulled up to his belly. One fist was thrust out on the ground in front of him. While I looked at him, the fist unclenched and the hand lay limp.

Johnny Angel was standing, staring. The other man was still gulping, lying, face down, with his head on his arm. When he wasn't gulping, he was sobbing.

Sobbing! I heaved him over. Carlos Angel was sobbing.

He was sorry he'd killed so many nice people.

Print-on-demand titles available at
CoachwhipBooks.com

Ebook titles available at
Coachwhip.com

ODDS-ON MURDER

DANCE

JACK DOLPH

murder is mutuel

JACK DOLPH

DEAD
WEIGHT

ADDISON
SIMMONS

DEATH
ON THE CAMPUS

ADDISON
SIMMONS

NARROW
GAUGE TO
MURDER

CAROLYN THOMAS

NOW I LAY ME
DOWN TO DIE

ELIZABETH TEBBETTS-TAYLOR

DEATH
OVER
NEWARK

ALEXANDER WILLIAMS

THE JINX
THEATRE
MURDER

ALEXANDER WILLIAMS

LADY
IN
LILAC

SUSANNAH SHANE

MURDER
IN THE
ROUGH

LESLIE
ALLEN

3
DETECTIVES
FEMMES AUDACIEUSES
MERWIN • SOMERVILLE • FOOTNER

3
DETECTIVES
MURDER
ON THE RAILS
WHITECHURCH • THORNE
• TORGERSON

THE
WINE ROOM
MURDER

STANLEY VESTAL

THE
WEEK–END
MYSTERY

ROBERT A. SIMON

THE EDINGTONS

THE HOUSE OF THE
VANISHING
GOBLETS

**THE GOLDFISH
MURDERS**

WILL MITCHELL